LULU
DARK

CAN SEE
THROUGH
WALLS

LULU DARK

CAN SEE THROUGH WALLS

A MYSTERY BY

BENNETT MADISON

SLEUTH
RAZORBILL

Lulu Dark Can See Through Walls

RAZORBILL

Published by the Penguin Group
Penguin Young Readers Group
345 Hudson Street, New York, New York 10014, U.S.A.
Penguin Group (USA) Inc., 375 Hudson Street, New York, New York 10014, U.S.A.
Penguin Books Canada Ltd, 10 Alcorn Avenue, Toronto, Ontario,
Canada M4V 3B2 (a division of Pearson Penguin Canada, Inc.)
Penguin Books Ltd, 80 Strand, London WC2R 0RL, England
Penguin Ireland, 25 St Stephen's Green, Dublin 2, Ireland
(a division of Penguin Books Ltd)
Penguin Group (Australia), 250 Camberwell Road, Camberwell,
Victoria 3124, Australia (a division of Pearson Australia Group Pty Ltd)
Penguin Books India Pvt Ltd, 11 Community Centre, Panchsheel Park,
New Delhi – 110 017, India
Penguin Group (NZ), Cnr Airborne and Rosedale Roads, Albany,
Auckland 1310, New Zealand (a division of Pearson New Zealand Ltd)
Penguin Books (South Africa) (Pty) Ltd, 24 Sturdee Avenue, Rosebank,
Johannesburg 2196, South Africa

Penguin Books Ltd, Registered Offices: 80 Strand, London WC2R 0RL, England

10 9 8 7 6 5 4 3 2 1

Interior design by Christopher Grassi

Library of Congress Cataloging-in-Publication Data

Madison, Bennett.
  Lulu Dark can see through walls / by Bennett Madison.
    p. cm.
  Summary: When someone steals her purse and her identity, high-school junior and reluctant girl sleuth
Lulu Dark investigates.
  ISBN 1-59514-010-7 (hardcover)
  [1. Identity theft—Fiction 2. Interpersonal relations—Fiction. 3. Mystery and detective stories.
4. Humorous stories.] I. Title.
  PZ7.M26Lu 2005
  [Fic]—dc22   2004026073

Printed in the United States of America

For the real Lulu Darks: Emily and Lucy.
You could both be nicer, but you could not be good-er.

ONE MY NAME IS LULU DARK. I AM NOT

the girl detective type.

I'm not going to name names, but I know a thing or two about those amateur sleuths, the ones you read about in books, and they couldn't be more different from me.

I do not speak Arabic or Chinese or German or even Spanish like they do. I speak English, and the only French phrases I know are things like, "I go to the beach," or, "We go to the pool, yes?" I don't do jujitsu, I don't have a photographic memory, and I've never skydived. I can't water-ski and I don't want to. If there was a criminal escaping on water skis with a satchel full of priceless diamonds, I would certainly not chase after her in any way. What I would do is yawn and be glad that they weren't my diamonds because for one thing, I don't have any diamonds. My dad has a lot of valuable paintings, but if an evil crook carried them off across a tightrope, it would be no big deal because he's a famous painter and he'd just paint some more. No death-defying pursuit necessary.

I'm not trying to be a jerk, but I believe in truth, and the truth is that if old Mrs. Banneker next door told me that her poor, beloved cat was missing, it wouldn't occur to me to be intrigued. I wouldn't say, "That sounds mysterious, Mrs. Banneker, I'll go investigate." Instead I would say, "That's too bad, Mrs. Banneker. Good thing you've still got fifteen cats left."

Of course, there's no old Mrs. Banneker next door anyway.

Please. What universe do these girl detectives live in? In fact, the apartment next door is occupied by this yuppie couple who have never even introduced themselves. God knows what their names are. One time, though, I did hear them having phone sex when the signals on our portable phones crossed. Then I went and took like the longest shower of my entire life.

You must be wondering why I'm telling you all this. I must sound like a total jerk, dissing on imaginary Mrs. Banneker and some yuppies I don't even know and . . . well, you probably know the girl detective's name.

Pardon me if I'm peevish, but you would be too if you'd found yourself hiding out in a Dumpster at three in the morning over some petty amateur sleuth crap that you did not—repeat, *not*—sign up for. But what can you do when the criminals are practically lining up to bug you, and I'm talking *you personally?* When you're a girl like me, you fight back. Which, of course, is how it all started.

It was a perfect moment. You know the type. That feeling you get every now and then when—just for a second—everything seems so ideal? Charlie, Daisy, and I were in our usual booth at Big Blonde—the slightly elevated one, right by the pool table. We were a little bit bored. It had been ages since anything interesting had happened, and I, for one, didn't have high hopes for the evening. We'd been having the same exact type of fun every Friday night for months. Why should this one be any different?

Well. It was.

We were at the club to see this band called the Many Handsomes, and apparently everyone else in Halo City had the same idea. The place was totally packed with people, including, it seemed, half the kids from Orchard Academy, where Daisy, Charlie, and I are juniors. Everyone was buzzing around, scoping each other out, doing their usual thing.

"This band is going to blow up, like, any day if this many people are on to them," Charlie said. "Is there anyone who's *not* here?"

I glanced around the room. Our booth had the best view in the whole place, and Charlie had a point. There were so many people at Big Blonde it was hard to pick any one person out of the crowd. It was a faceless throng—my favorite kind. But as I let my gaze drift through the mass, I started to recognize a few faces—one by one, and then more.

Adam Wahl, Charlie's friend, was sitting at the coffee bar with all the other guys from the jazz band, and Trina Rockwell and Blair Wright, the two most popular girls in the school, were standing by the bathrooms, examining themselves in the mirrors of their compacts while they gossiped with each other.

"Look," Charlie said. "Even Berlin is here."

Berlin Silver had just transferred to our school in January. When

Charlie mentioned her, I followed the direction of his gaze, peering over the rims of my glasses.

Berlin was standing by the jukebox, studying the selection and shaking her butt in an approximation of rhythm. She was blond and leggy and practically as tall as me, which was nice because it made me feel like less of an overgrown freak.

"Ugh," Daisy groaned, shaking her head ruefully at the sight of Berlin. "Berlin Silver has a terrible case of the vile juju. Beware. Wherever she goes, only trouble can follow. It is a matter of bad karma."

I laughed. "You're mixing your mysticisms. Karma or juju: you only get to pick one. And I don't see why you have such a problem with Berlin. What has she ever done to you?"

"Nothing. That's the point. Neither of you guys notice it because she sucks up to you. *You* both have money and important parents. But when it comes to a scholarship student, she has no reason to acknowledge me at all. I don't think she's ever uttered a word in my direction."

Daisy likes almost everyone, so I always listen up when she has a nasty feeling about someone. In this case, I felt bad. I hate it when the snobbier people at our private school treat Daisy differently because she's not, like, a sultan's daughter or something.

"I'll take your word for it," I told her. "Sorry I never noticed. No one gets away with being a jerk to my friends."

Charlie was listening to the conversation, taking it all in with careful consideration. He looked across the crowd at Berlin appraisingly. "I'll tell you one thing," he said. "Snob or not, that girl is hot."

"Whatever," I replied. "She's just your usual run-of-the-mill blonde."

Berlin had turned from the jukebox and was dancing all by herself. She was wearing a blue sequined tube top and skintight black pants. She had her hands over her head and was hopping from side to side, swaying precariously on her enormous espadrilles. It was a weird dance, but I had to admit it was sort of cute.

"It's a fact." Charlie shrugged. "There's not a guy at school who's not into her."

"Except you." Daisy ribbed him with her elbow. "Right?"

"Right," he said unconvincingly.

I twirled a chunk of hair around my pinky. "It is funny how she doesn't quite fit in, though," I mused. "Think about it. She's rich, well dressed, and pretty. It seems like the perfect formula for head-cheerleader-style popularity. But aside from having the boys drooling, she's not exactly the queen of Orchard Academy."

"Well, she is a little weird," Charlie pointed out. "And all she ever talks about is how her great-grandfather invented the aluminum can."

"It's like she learned how to be a person from watching *Dynasty* reruns on cable," I agreed.

"Exactly," Daisy said. "As a matter of fact, I predict that she's only here because French *Vogue* says this band is fashionable."

"I canceled my French *Vogue* subscription, so I wouldn't know," I said. "But you have to admit they're on to something. Look around. Everyone in this room can tell that something big is going to happen tonight."

I was sort of right, it turned out, although in the end it didn't have much to do with the band.

The three of us scanned the crowd together, taking it all in. It was nice to be just the three of us, all calm and easy in the middle of that pandemonium.

Then Daisy whispered, "Don't flip out, Lulu. Your favorite people are here."

I groaned. Daisy didn't have to say the words. I knew exactly who she meant.

Rachel Buttersworth-Taylor and Marisol Bloom were making their way into the place, glued to each other as usual. They tossed their ponytails around, laughing and chatting up everyone they saw.

Even though they're my total enemies, there was such a good vibe in the club that I almost smiled when I saw them working the crowd. I caught myself just in time, though, holding my frown and rolling my eyes. When you have enemies, it's important not to go soft about them.

"Lulu." Daisy's voice was firm. "No fighting with Rachel Buttersworth-Taylor tonight. Okay?"

"Maybe you should try liking them," Charlie suggested. "They actually can be somewhat cool."

"What?" I snapped, annoyed. "You want me to like them? This feud with Rachel and Marisol isn't even my fault. You both know that!"

It's so silly to think about now, but it all started over a boy.

Rachel and I have known each other since kindergarten, but we haven't always been enemies. In fact, we never paid much attention to each other at all until seventh grade, when she started "going with" this guy named Sam Mason. That's what you call it in seventh grade because you're obviously not *going out*. There's no *out* to go to—except for maybe the playground, which isn't all that romantic.

Anyway, Rachel and Sam went together for a week, and then he got bored with her and started going with *me*. It was so not a big deal. It's not like I stole him. No one dates for more than a week in seventh grade anyway.

Before the end of the year Sam's family moved to Los Angeles, which is probably just as well. But the point is that Rachel totally freaked out over the whole thing, claiming that *I* snatched her boyfriend. That's where the whole war started.

Hello? It was seventh grade! Who cares? But if she was going to start trouble, I wasn't going to take it lying down.

I guess it all got a little bit out of hand.

"Listen." I sighed, pleading my case to Daisy and Charlie. "I've tried to bury the hatchet with Rachel many times and it just doesn't work. She's the one with the issue. And in case you don't recall, may I remind you of the fishy little episode she pulled with one of our friends from the sea—"

"As if you'd ever let us forget," Charlie cut me off. "Never mind that it was over two years ago."

I started to protest, but Daisy placed a warning hand on my knee.

"Brace yourself," she said. "The dreaded ones approach."

I watched in horror as Rachel and Marisol headed toward our table, then put on my hardest drop-dead face. I may not be the most popular girl in school, but I make up for it by being pretty intimidating when I want to. Marisol and Rachel just wanted to stir things up. Well, they could try their hardest, because nothing was going to faze me tonight.

"Hey, guys," Rachel said sweetly when they got to our booth. Marisol stood by her side with her trademark fake-shy smirk.

Of the two, only Rachel was openly evil, but sometimes I thought that quiet little Marisol was the truly scary one. I don't trust people who pretend to be shy. You can just see the wheels turning in their heads as they plot all their sneaky little schemes.

"Hey, Rachel," Charlie replied. "What are you guys up to tonight?"

I scowled at him. He's so friendly that he can't help being pals with everyone. Traitor.

"We're here for the show. I've been into the Many Handsomes, like, forever," Rachel said. "Since way before anyone else heard of them." She turned to me just in time to catch me rolling my eyes. She gave me a mean, squinty grin. And although I tried very hard, I couldn't suppress a small, sarcastic snort.

Rachel's eyes were stony. "Lulu," she said snarkily, "don't you have, like, a dermatologist's appointment you should be at or something? You've had that zit on your jaw for like a week now."

I felt my face flush. I didn't think anyone had noticed my zit—I'd been doing such a good job of covering it up!

"You should be so lucky, Rachel," I fumed. "I'd rather have a huge, rancid zit than be cursed with a face like yours."

An ominous cloud darkened Rachel's eyes, and Marisol glanced nervously at her friend to see how she would react. In the end they couldn't think up a comeback.

Both girls turned tail, making a beeline for the front of the stage. In my mind, I chalked up another point for myself. No one gets the best of Lulu Dark.

"Very charming, Lulu," Daisy grumbled after they had gone. "Can't you just ignore them?"

I tried to look contrite, but it's really not my strongest suit.

"Hey!" I protested. "They were the ones picking on me!" My friends paid no attention.

"I'm going to get another cup of coffee," Charlie said. He got up and mussed his hair self-consciously, looking both ways to see if anyone was checking him out. Daisy and I both saw him do it. We exchanged a glance.

"What?" Charlie asked.

"Nothing," we said together, stifling giggles.

"Charlie's such a social butterfly," I whispered when he was out of earshot. "He just wants to see and be seen. It's probably the reason he goes through girlfriends so fast. He can't help being a flirt."

"I think he gets it from his mom and his sister," Daisy replied.

She was right. Carly and Genevieve Reed are the reigning social queens of their respective age groups in Halo City. Carly, his mom, is always throwing these huge charity benefits, which are really just excuses for all her socialite friends to buy new gowns. His sister, Genevieve, on the other hand, skips through the downtown haunts of the well-heeled, abusing cocktail waiters and leaving a trail of broken hearts, unpaid tabs, and stubbed-out Capris.

I thought about it for a second. By all rights Charlie should have turned out to be another bratty trustafarian. But instead he's a nice guy to the core.

"Have you noticed that it's been sort of a while since Charlie's dated anyone?" I asked.

Daisy shrugged. "I guess. Maybe he's just . . ."

She paused, distracted, then giggled in bewilderment. "Lulu, check out that girl in the corner."

I turned around and immediately hooted. About ten feet away from us a bored, mean-looking girl in *sunglasses* leaned up against the wall. She whipped out a bottle of nail polish and began painting her nails.

"What is she doing?" I asked, totally confused. "Why would anyone come to a packed club just to work on her manicure? And is she for real with those sunglasses?"

"Good questions," Daisy said. "Maybe she's an albino with obsessive-compulsive disorder. Or perhaps she's an employee of

Sally Hansen, the nail polish company." She tapped a finger on her chin, taking the issue very seriously. "That doesn't explain the sunglasses, though."

"Maybe she *is* Sally Hansen!" I mused. "She's wearing the sunglasses because she doesn't want to be seen by her adoring fans!"

"You know, I always wondered who Sally Hansen really was," Daisy said, slipping into her own universe. "I've often thought she might be the illegitimate daughter of Estée Lauder—abandoned on some church doorstep in Wisconsin and taken in by Norwegian immigrants."

"Well, if that *is* her, we should make friends." I giggled. "Maybe she'll give us free polish."

"Better that than Wet 'n' Wild," Daisy decided. "But I wouldn't count on being best buddies. She looks kind of, um, forbidding."

At that moment Sally Hansen looked up from her nails and glared right at us. Daisy and I quickly averted our eyes, studying our coffee cups like they were the most fascinating things in the world.

Whew! Nearly caught mid-mockery. That was a close one.

I swirled my mug around, watching the black stuff inside slide back and forth. Sometimes I think my coffee would taste better if I put milk and sugar and all that junk into it, but my dad taught me from a young age that to do that would be wrong. I took a final, bitter swig.

"Did Charlie say that he was going to get me more?" I asked.

"He didn't mention it," Daisy answered.

I realized that Charlie had actually been gone for a while. "Where has that boy gotten to?" I wondered aloud.

"Bathroom, maybe?" Daisy guessed. But for some reason I didn't think so.

"I'll bet you anything that Berlin Silver has him cornered. She's just itching for a date with Charlie."

"Definitely," Daisy said, making a face. "You should see how she stares at him in study hall. Like a wolf about to devour a helpless little lamb. Or a puppy. A *beagle* puppy."

"I'll go see if he needs rescuing."

"You do that," Daisy said.

I pulled my purse onto my lap and snapped it open. It was my favorite purse—a fake Kate Spade that I bought from an extra-shady bootlegger on the corner of Roxbury and Flower Avenue. I'd had it for two years, and the way I was attached to it, I can't even tell you.

It had a garish, tacky, pink-and-yellow flower pattern and a hot pink strap. I loved it precisely because it *was* a phony and because—with its ridiculously over-the-top design—it looked like no other bag in the world.

I grabbed my lip gloss from inside and slicked on a new coat. Then I tossed the bag over my shoulder and made my way through the crush of the crowd.

When I found Charlie, he was pushed up against a wall by the bathroom, and what do you know: Berlin Silver was leaning in close, making doe eyes at him. Her sparkly tube top was pulled up just enough to reveal the silver tattoo on her hip bone. It's a shark, and Berlin is obviously very proud of it. She makes sure to wear skimpy clothes that show it off just so everyone knows how hard-core she is, even though I suspect that she's secretly kind of a pushover.

I couldn't hear what she was saying over the din of the opening band, but I could guess: she was telling him about how cool she was, or how rich her dad is, or about the genius design of the aluminum can. When it comes to conversation, Berlin Silver is kind of predictable.

"Charlie," I said with a breezy smile, squeezing in between the two of them. "How did I know I'd find you talking to Berlin?"

He grimaced sarcastically. "I don't know, Lulu. Maybe your famous x-ray vision?"

He turned to Berlin with an apologetic slant to his eyebrows. "Lulu Dark can see through walls, you know. She knows everything that goes on in Halo City."

"Gee, Lulu. You're, like, a superhero," Berlin cooed, glancing down at her own cleavage and sneakily adjusting her tube top.

I couldn't decide why I was suddenly so annoyed with Berlin. Maybe I was just mad at her for being such a snob to Daisy. Unlike Charlie, I'm not easily wooed by people who are mean to my friends.

"I *am* like a superhero," I told Berlin. "But I don't see through walls. I see through people." I gave a half smile, half scowl, and Berlin withdrew a little, taken aback.

"Don't listen to her, Berlin," Charlie said. "She's just in a funk."

Berlin laughed long and loud, even though Charlie hadn't said anything particularly hilarious.

She sort of sounds like that woman from The Nanny *when she laughs,* I decided. On the other hand, I've been told that my laugh sounds like whale song, so maybe I'm not one to talk.

"Whatever," Berlin chirped. "Don't worry, Lulu, I know you didn't mean anything."

I was about to tell her I *did* mean it, but Charlie had already grabbed me by the purse strap to drag me away. The Many Handsomes were busy setting up their crap, and Daisy was beckoning from the spot she'd staked out at the edge of the stage.

"Lulu," Charlie said as we elbowed our way toward her, "just for tonight could you try not to live up to your reputation as an überbitch? Why can't you just be the nice person that I know you are?"

"Sorry," I retorted, "but what's with this crowd? First Rachel and Marisol pick on me, and then Berlin acts like she's your girlfriend. I feel like I'm at a convention for the obnoxious. And when in Rome, right?"

"Whatever." Charlie sighed.

The thing is, I knew he was right. Sometimes it's just easier for me to be mean because it's so much worse to be defenseless. Around here they put ketchup on nice girls and serve them for lunch. That's one of the only valuable things my mother taught me—before she moved to California to be a C-list starlet.

Even so, I didn't want Charlie to think of me as an "überbitch"— or even the regular kind. I don't know why I cared what he thought. It just mattered. He was so innocent, like a little bunny rabbit. He didn't understand why it was sometimes safer to be like a porcupine instead.

"Where'd you find him?" Daisy wanted to know when we got to the stage.

"Berlin was hoping Charlie would propose marriage," I teased. "She was practically slobbering over the thought of a make-out session in his dad's jet."

"Give her a break," he said. "She's just trying to make friends. She's the same way with you, isn't she?"

I had to give him that one.

"I just hate that Berlin tries so hard," I decided. "I mean, she's so freaky. Can't she make friends like a normal, non-deranged person?" When I got to the end of the sentence, Daisy's eyes had widened at me. She was tight-lipped, shaking her head in a tiny little *no*.

"What?" I said. "You hate her a lot more than I do."

Her expression grew more dire. I swung my head around . . . and found Berlin. She was standing right behind me—her eyes wide and her mouth formed into the *O* of surprise. Our eyes met, and she looked like she was either about to cry or kill me.

"Oops," I said halfheartedly. She turned and walked away.

Ugh! I felt terrible. Why did things like that always have to happen to me? I wasn't trying to hurt anyone's feelings. I was just saying the first thing that popped into my head. I barely even meant any of it.

We watched as Berlin stalked her way through the crowd, knocking over at least a few drinks as she went. She was almost at the door when she stopped, reconsidered, and turned around. Berlin made her way over to the corner, where Sally Hansen was standing, still working on her manicure. She appeared to strike up a conversation.

"Whoa," said Daisy. "I guess weirdos stick together."

But Charlie wasn't having it. "I don't see what's so weird," he said. "You guys shouldn't—"

Luckily, before Charlie could launch into a full-on lecture, the band launched into their first song. It was this totally kicky number with hand claps and lots of *la la la*s. I'm a sucker for anything with *la la la*s, and when I started dancing, I was instantly in a good mood again.

After the first song I took a second to look at the band—and almost lost it for real. The Many Handsomes lived up to their name, and the lead singer was the best of all of them. He was tall and sinewy and totally jacked, with black, wavy hair, blue eyes, and tan skin—like the statue of David if he wore tight jeans and a black tank top. He was playing his guitar with revved-up gusto, biting his lip, veins and muscles popping.

I leaned over to Daisy and did my best to whisper, even though we were right by the speakers. "Who on earth is that singer?"

"His name's Alfy Romero," Daisy said. "Didn't you read his profile in last week's *YM?*" I shook my head, then turned back toward the band. Daisy continued in my ear. "If you think he looks cute in a tank top, you should see him in a bathing suit."

The music grew more intense, and I let it sweep me up, up, up.

I was getting into the groove to an embarrassing degree when Alfy Romero looked down and flashed me a smile that could have powered all of Halo City. I tried to be cool, meeting his gaze and letting the corner of my mouth tilt the tiniest bit. But it was hard not to melt. I was disarmed, and let me tell you, it takes a lot to throw *me* off.

It could have been my imagination, but I swear he held the look for the rest of the song, and when it was over, I elbowed Daisy excitedly. "Did you see that?" I asked while Alfy studied the set list.

She grinned and raised her eyebrows. "Everyone saw it," she said. "Marisol and Rachel are green with envy." She gestured over at the girls, who had unfortunately wound up a foot or two away from us in the pogoing mob, arms folded dyspeptically across their chests.

Charlie had noticed too, I guess.

"Will you two give it a rest?" he grumbled. "You're acting like giggly little schoolgirls."

"We *are* schoolgirls," Daisy said. "And you're acting like a jealous boyfriend."

"Jealous! What do I have to be jealous about?"

"Maybe you have a little crush on Lulu yourself."

"Ha!" I exclaimed.

"Get real, Daisy," Charlie said with a scowl. "Lulu and I took baths together when we were babies. Having a crush on her would be like having a crush on my sister."

"Except that your sister's an evil fink," I pointed out, slightly offended by the comparison.

"Well, at least my sister doesn't burp all the time, like you do."

Daisy listened to us, swinging her head back and forth like she was watching a tennis match. "Please, you two," she interrupted. "This is too much. If I wanted to watch a Meg Ryan movie, I would have gone out with my mom tonight."

"Shut up, Daisy," Charlie mumbled, totally blushing at this point.

"Fine. I'll say no more," Daisy shouted above the music. "Let's just be happy for Lulu. Mr. Many Handsomes is quite smitten!"

"What was that you just said?" the eavesdropping Rachel Buttersworth-Taylor interjected.

"Nothing," Daisy told her. Too bad Daisy is a terrible liar. I'm pretty bad myself, which is why I never lie, not even white ones.

"That's funny," Rachel said, her eyes sparkling wickedly. "I thought you just told Charlie that Alfy Romero has a crush on Lulu."

"Um, no. Uh-uh. Not at all." Daisy shook her head emphatically, which made her seem even less convincing.

"Well, just remember, Lulu has a tendency to imagine things like that," Rachel began, going in for the kill. "Remember when she thought that Mr. Adams, the Latin teacher, was in love with her— and then he gave her a D?"

I gasped. It was a cheap shot. Plus it was so obvious that the reason he gave me a D was because he was trying to throw everyone off the truth.

Unfortunately, bringing *that* up wouldn't exactly help my case.

I was at a loss for an original comeback, so I went for a low blow of my own. "No way, Rachel. Your head's all screwy. Must be all the boozing your mom did when you were in the womb."

Rachel's smirk disappeared. Her eyes turned to steel. Even though the band was playing louder than ever and the crowd was going crazy, you could feel the air escaping from the little circle we were standing in.

For the first time that night Marisol spoke up. "You know what, Lulu? You're a real piece of work." She took Rachel by the hand to usher her away, then turned back for a final retort. "You should be ashamed of yourself."

I'll be honest: it's not like what she said was devastating or anything, but something about her icy tone gave me goose bumps.

Daisy turned, grabbed my shoulders, and practically shook me. "Lulu!" she scolded. "That was not cool. Just because you know the most hurtful thing to say doesn't mean you always have to say it."

I frowned in confusion. "What's the big deal? On the Richter scale of insults, what I said barely even registers."

"You don't remember?" Daisy asked.

"Remember what?"

"The time Rachel's mom showed up sloshed to the eighth-grade potluck dinner? Rachel's sensitive about that stuff!"

"Oh," I said. "Right."

Truthfully, I didn't remember the potluck dinner at all. Then it occurred to me—eighth grade was the year I had mono. I probably missed the entire thing.

A strange, hollow feeling settled in my stomach. I hadn't been trying to do any *real* damage. I do have some decency. It's like, I only make fun of people for being fat if they're totally skinny. You don't want to cut too close to the bone; otherwise you end up looking like a jerk.

But Rachel and I are always bickering, I told myself. There was nothing to do now except put it all out of my mind. For the rest of the evening I tried hard not to think about what I had said. Dwelling on it gave me a bad case of guilt-induced anxiety.

The music the band was playing was shaking me from the inside out, humming with a warm, dreamy drunkenness. I felt it in my knees and lungs, and I closed my eyes, letting the thrill of the room blanket me. There it was again: another glimpse of the perfect.

I was still stuck in it twenty minutes later when the Many Handsomes' last song ended. It took a couple of seconds of listening to the crowd going wild for me to realize that the set was over.

The stage lights blinked off, and I was struggling to see when I felt a tap on my shoulder from above. My heart somersaulted when I realized that I was face-to-face with Alfy Romero.

He was bent down, leaning over at me from the stage. All I could make out was the vague outline of his chiseled jaw, his perfect lips. His breath, which didn't even smell bad, grazed my cheek. He put his hand on my shoulder. I nearly swooned.

"This one," he called to someone in the wings.

For once I was dumbstruck. I opened my mouth to speak and realized that I had no idea what to say.

It didn't matter, though. A second later the stage lights faded back on.

As the rest of the band returned to the stage, Alfy stood up and strapped on his guitar for the encore. He stood wide-legged in a warrior stance, bounced once, and strummed a big, echoing power chord before the drums and the bass kicked in.

When the show was over, we were sweaty and breathless, glowing with energy. I was still getting my bearings when a big guy in a dirty T-shirt and cargo shorts came sidling up next to me.

"From Alfy Romero," he said. He handed me a piece of folded-up paper before shuffling off to the stage door.

Surreptitiously I looked down and unfolded the paper he'd handed me. It was the Many Handsomes' set list, printed in messy, boyish, Sharpie scrawl. At the bottom a note: *You're beautiful,* it read, in the same adorable chicken scratch. *Call me. XOXO Alfy R.* Then—prize of all prizes—his phone number! I gasped and stuffed it quickly into my purse.

Suddenly I felt eyes on me. Daisy and Charlie were both staring.

"Lulu," Daisy said, slack-jawed. "You are brilliant! How did you make that happen?"

I shrugged. It was a total mystery to me.

Charlie shook his head. "I hope you're not actually considering calling him. I mean, musicians will give their numbers to anything in heels."

My smile quickly evaporated. "But I'm wearing hot pink cowboy boots!" I argued weakly.

"Charlie, don't be such a jerk," Daisy stepped in. "It's obvious that Alfy noticed Lulu because she's one of a kind and he happened to be nervy enough to do something about it!"

"Whatever," Charlie said. "Believe what you want to believe. I'm outta here."

"You're not going to stay for another coffee?" I asked.

"Nah, I promised my sister I'd take her dog for a walk before I went to bed." He gave us each a quick kiss on the cheek, zipped up his sweatshirt, and booked for the door.

I was still trying to figure out what to make of the situation when I heard a giggle behind me and felt a cold wetness on my butt.

"Oops!" came a shrill, familiar chirp. I twirled around. No surprise; it was Rachel and Marisol again. Rachel was clutching an empty glass to her chest, barely hiding her jubilance.

"What the hell . . . ?" I exclaimed, craning my neck to survey the back of my skirt. A huge wet spot was quickly spreading across my butt. In a second I knew what had happened. Rachel had accidentally on purpose spilled her iced coffee all over my favorite pink-fringed vintage skirt! It was dripping down my legs—and into my cowboy boots!

"I'm *so* sorry, Lulu." Rachel snickered. "I can be such a klutz sometimes. Don't worry, though, the iced coffee blends right in with the pattern."

Marisol was standing behind her friend, looking amused but sort of embarrassed.

No time for arguments. The clock was ticking. I beckoned urgently to Daisy.

Daisy took one look at the sludge dripping down the backs of my legs and flew to my rescue. "Quick," she said, shooting Rachel and

Marisol a reproving glance. "If we work fast, we might be able to salvage your skirt!"

We rushed to the bar, where she swiped a pitcher of water and some napkins and got to work cleaning.

It was a lost cause; I could tell from the start. I loved my poor little fringed skirt. I'd bought it at a flea market for only five dollars. Now it was gone.

A small part of me realized that maybe I had it coming.

"Sorry, Lu," Daisy said after a valiant effort. "I don't think there's much more I can do. If only I could remember that Swedish trick with the egg whites and tonic water that my mother taught me. . . ."

"It's fine." I shrugged. "Just clothes, right?"

"That's the spirit," Daisy cheered. "Let's go. We are so done with this place." She made a move for the door.

"Wait!" I exclaimed, patting myself down. "What did I do with my purse?"

"Don't panic," Daisy said. "You probably left it on the stage."

"Right," I answered. "Follow me."

We waded against the exiting crowd toward the area of the stage where Alfy Romero first fell under my spell. We were nearly there when the girl we'd dubbed Sally Hansen emerged in front of us.

She narrowed her eyes when she caught sight of me.

"Cow," she murmured under her breath, leaning close to whisper in my ear. Then on her way by she slammed her shoulder into mine, coming close to knocking me over.

"Whoa," Daisy breathed.

Then as quickly as she appeared, Sally Hansen was gone—lost in the crowd.

"Weird," I said, disconcerted to say the least. "What did I ever do to her?"

Daisy shrugged. "You're just not making any friends tonight."

"Except Alfy!" I winked at her.

We reached the stage and glanced around for my purse. There were a few discarded cups, some crumpled flyers, and a puddle of unidentifiable liquid but nothing close to a handbag anywhere in sight.

I searched harder, looking for any sign of the telltale pattern. Still nothing. "My purse!" I yelped. "I know I left it here!"

A terrible thought occurred to both me and Daisy at the same time. "Alfy Romero's phone number!" we exclaimed together.

We dropped to all fours and scoured the floor. Then we ran to our booth and dug into the seat cushions.

But it was no use.

The number, along with my purse, was gone.

That was the beginning. If I was any sort of girl detective, I would have seen it coming.

TWO ON SATURDAY IN DAGGER PARK,

the neighborhood where Rachel Buttersworth-Taylor lives, the jammed tree-lined sidewalks were filled with little dogs and fifty-something ladies wearing tailored black suits. Everywhere you looked, the place glittered with platinum-streaked coifs, huge, garish pins, and the glinty eyes of silver-haired men.

It was noon, the morning after my purse was stolen. Daisy and I had jetted up there, to the northwest corner of Halo City, to give Rachel the shakedown. After what had happened the night before, I was more than positive that she'd taken it, either for revenge or because she wanted Alfy Romero's phone number for herself.

It was probably a combination of the two—though I don't know what she would have done with that number. If Alfy had wanted to give his number to a fink like her, he would have, so what's the point in stealing?

Anyway, it was a yellowish spring day, and the sunlight bursting through a leafy filter gave the streets in Dagger Park an aspect of unreality—like they'd been built for Disney World or something.

Daisy and I were standing outside Rachel's house, where she lived with her mom.

Casa Buttersworth-Taylor is a tricked-out old town house with a big oak door and ivy crawling the walls. Daisy and I found ourselves staring at that door together. We'd come all this way, and now neither of us wanted to push the buzzer.

"You do it," Daisy said. "It's your purse."

"No, you do it. Rachel hates you less. Maybe I'll just hide here in this shrub." I gestured nervously at a tiny neon azalea at the foot of the granite stoop.

"No way," Daisy scoffed. "If this is happening, you're going to have to be the one to do the deed."

I hesitated. Much as I hated to admit it, Rachel was a worthy foe. She had a crazy recklessness that I almost—that's *almost*—admired. Who else would have had not only the nerve but the straight-up, messed-up, evil spark to pull that trick with the dead fish?

It happened freshman year, during the school production of *Fiddler on the Roof*. Because our school's so small, participation in the stupid play was always mandatory. Daisy, Charlie, and I all wound up in the chorus, which ironically is where they stick everyone who can't carry a tune. Basically, if you're in the chorus, you just stand around a lot with some kind of prop—in my case a bottle of Manischewitz (empty, unfortunately)—and you sort of sway and mumble along while everyone else is singing. Sometimes you have to do really humiliating stuff like skip around in a circle and curtsy fifty times in a row, but in general, chorus seemed like the best place to be. I was so mortified to be in a lame school musical in the first place that as far as I was concerned, the tinier the part, the better.

Rachel, on the other hand, was beyond peeved to have landed such a meaningless role. Apparently she had decided that she was going to be a famous actress—never mind the fact that she had a face like a Thoroughbred.

She'd assumed all along that the lead was hers, no prob. But when the parts were posted, she hadn't even gotten a speaking role. Rachel informed everyone that it was just as well, that she needed to save her voice for commercial auditions anyway, but you could tell she was crying on the inside.

Personally, I always sort of wished Rachel *had* gotten to be the star, because it would have been a riot watching her try to sing. Daisy and I listened at the door during her audition and it turned out that Rachel Buttersworth-Taylor was the only person I knew who could sing "The Wind Beneath My Wings" to the same tune as "Row, Row, Row Your Boat."

Anyway, Rachel hated me already, and she'd pretty much been shut out of her dreams of school-play stardom, so you can imagine her total rage when, somehow, I wound up with a line instead of her.

One stupid line! All I got to do was run across the stage, twirl, and shout, "L'chaim—to life!" during the wedding scene, but the fact that Mr. Milford picked *me* to do it was about as much as Rachel could take. If Mr. Milford had, you know, *asked me,* I would definitely have turned it down, but when I suggested that to Rachel, she looked at me like she'd caught me picking my nose.

So then, the day after Mr. Milford picked me, in the dressing room I opened up my backpack to find *a real live dead fish* in it.

It was jammed haphazardly into the math section of my binder. Seriously. It still had scales on it and eyeballs and everything.

There was a note too, written in red lipstick on my laboriously plagiarized precalculus homework: *LULU DARK SMELLS LIKE TUNA.*

I was horrified, of course, but unfortunately, I had to admit, at that moment it was true.

The day the incident occurred, I clenched my fist with resolve and swore that nothing Rachel Buttersworth-Taylor ever did would make me shrink from conflict. Standing on her doorstep, however, I found myself reconsidering. If the girl had resorted to thievery, perhaps she was a person built without the limits of decency. Who knew what she would do if I set her off again?

Then I thought of my purse. Sure, it was only a fake Kate Spade, and I barely had anything in it when it was stolen—I'd been carrying my cell phone and cash in my boot because it had seemed like the tough thing to do—but I loved that bag more than anything in the universe! And then there was that phone number—*Alfy's* phone number. The magical digits that were going to set my love life on fire.

The thought that Rachel might manage to sabotage my chance at true love made me so furious that all rationality gave way. I was going to get my purse back if I had to take a canoe to China to do it.

I marched up the stairs and jammed my finger into the doorbell, ready to face whatever Rachel could dish out.

But when the door swung open, I found myself faced not with Rachel, but the infamous Mrs. Taylor herself. She was wearing a pink designer sweat suit that was unzipped to display her suspiciously buoyant décolletage. Her yellow hair was piled on top of her head in a glamorous bird's nest, and she was wearing high-heeled mules.

With her free hand Mrs. Taylor was clutching a large silver goblet that looked like it had been plundered from some South Sea pirate's booty.

She didn't seem surprised to see us. She flashed us a huge grin. "Please tell me you're selling Girl Scout cookies," she said in a lazy drawl. "Things just haven't been the same since I ran out of Thin Mints in December. I told my daughter to find some more on eBay, but I'm afraid she's just no good with computers."

I blinked. I hadn't considered the possibility that Rachel herself wouldn't answer the door. Now, faced with a crazy woman, I had no clue what to do or say!

Desperate, I looked around for Daisy. I found her lingering by the azalea—setting herself up for a quick getaway. Luckily once she saw my panic, her sense of loyalty kicked in.

"Hi, Mrs. Taylor," she said brightly. "We're here to see Rachel."

"Oh!" Mrs. Taylor's grin turned quickly to a sad frown. "No cookies at all?"

"I'm afraid not," Daisy apologized.

"Well, that's okay." Mrs. Taylor sighed. "Come on in, gals, I just love meeting Rachel's schoolmates." She beckoned to us, and as we followed, she danced peppily from the foyer into the living room. She plopped herself down on a lavish, velvet-looking couch and threw her high heels up onto the coffee table, which was downright covered in fancy knickknacks. As we watched in a daze, she wedged her feet, crossed at the ankles, in between crystal swans and little jewel-encrusted eggs and candle-less candlesticks and beckoned for us to sit. Daisy and I exchanged a look and gingerly lowered ourselves onto adjacent throne-like seats. I felt weird; the room reminded me of a much, much fancier version of my nana Dark's good living room, which no one was allowed to use and where all the furniture was perpetually covered in plastic. For a moment I had a good mind to reprimand Mrs. Taylor—to tell her to for God's sake take her feet off the coffee table. But I held my tongue.

We sat there in uncomfortable silence for what seemed like forever, while Mrs. Taylor just sipped her drink and smiled at us expectantly. Finally Daisy spoke up.

"So," she said, "can we talk to Rachel?"

"Rachel?"

"Yes, Rachel. Your daughter," I said pointedly. Mrs. Taylor looked hurt and I kicked myself for letting my sass show. Why couldn't I ever get a handle on it?

"Rachel's not here," Mrs. Taylor said. She seemed confused that she had to explain such a thing. "Today is Saturday. She's at her father's. Now tell me about yourselves, girls. What did you say your names were?"

"Um." I could feel myself blushing. "I'm Lulu Dark."

"I'm Daisy." Daisy reached out a hand to shake, and bafflingly, the woman took it and gave her a regal peck on the knuckle.

"Well, hello," she said with mild surprise, as if she had just realized that we were there.

"Nice to meet you, Mrs. Taylor," I said.

She winked. "Please. No need for formalities among friends. You can call me Tupper." Then she stood. "What's your pleasure, ladies?" she asked, placing her hands on her hips. "A little sherry, perhaps?"

I cleared my throat. Didn't she know that the drinking age had been twenty-one for like a million years? It wasn't like I hadn't tried my share of alcohol, but it was still totally bizarre for someone's mother to be offering it—at one o'clock in the afternoon.

"I'd love a Diet Coke," Daisy spoke up.

"Me too," I quickly offered.

"You young people and your soft drinks." Tupper laughed. "They get you all sugared up, you know. They make you wacky. Rachel's the same way, of course. She thinks it helps maintain her figure. But girls like you don't need to be thinking about that." She was still talking to us even though she'd moved on to the kitchen.

"I think she's tipsy," Daisy whispered urgently.

"No!" I gave Daisy my *duh* face. This lady was drunk as a skunk. It was kind of embarrassing. The only time I'd ever seen my dad drunk was a few Thanksgivings ago at Nana Dark's house. He'd ended the dinner going on and on about the aesthetic perfection of stuffed turkey. "It's just so unspeakably gorgeous," he kept saying over and over. I wanted to crawl under the table and hide till Christmas. I couldn't imagine what it would be like if he was that way all the time.

"Now I know why Rachel got so upset last night," I said.

"I told you. Sometimes I think you have Tourette's syndrome, or ESP, or some kind of evil combination of the two. I don't know how you know exactly the worst thing to say at any given moment, but you do."

I grimaced and decided to take Daisy's advice under consideration. Maybe it was time for some self-improvement. While I was at it, I could join a gym and stop eating fast food, too. But none of that was going to happen until I got my purse back.

As I was setting my mind on my real goal—handbag retrieval—Tupper skipped back into the room, carrying two more goblets, which she handed to me and Daisy. I got straight to the point.

"The reason we're here, Tupper," I said in my best grown-up voice, "is because I think Rachel may have picked up my purse last night. By accident, of course. Did you see her with it? It's a Kate Spade knockoff with an incredibly loud pink-and-yellow pattern."

"Oh no, dear," Mrs. Taylor said, looking thoughtful. "She got home so late, you know. But I'm sure she wouldn't mind if you took a little peek in her room. I know how it is for a lady to lose her handbag. Just pulverizing, really." She sat up straighter and smiled, obviously happy to be helpful.

I nodded seriously. I saw Daisy open her mouth to speak and—certain that she was going to decline the offer—rushed to cut her off. "I'd love to take a look," I said sweetly, then added with somber meaning: "I've got all my important lady things in there."

Daisy looked at me with reproach, but it was too late. I waited for Mrs. Taylor to lead the way to Rachel's room, but she had settled in on the couch again—this time sprawled out lengthwise. "By all means, go ahead," Mrs. Taylor said. "It's the first door on your left on the third floor. I'd show you, but I just hate climbing all those stairs." She leaned her head back and closed her eyes.

I hadn't come all this way just to kibitz with Tupper Taylor, so I hopped out of my seat and headed for the foyer with Daisy trailing.

"Lulu," Daisy whispered as we made our way up the wide, spiraling stairway, "this is totally uncool. We don't have any proof that Rachel took your purse. We can't just go snooping around in her room like we're the KGB. Stalinism is *so* not okay."

"If you're too chicken, you can wait outside," I told her, flinging open the door and marching into the enemy's lair.

Daisy grumbled, hovering on the threshold. "The only reason I'm up here is to keep an eye on you."

I glanced around Rachel's room, which was spotlessly clean and decorated in funky, bright colors. I didn't see my purse anywhere, but that didn't mean anything. If she was smart, she would have hidden it. I made a move to open her dresser, but that was where Daisy drew the line. Quick as a flash, she flung herself in front of me, arms spread, blocking the drawers.

"Lulu," Daisy said firmly. "That's going too far. Even if Rachel did steal your purse, we can't take the law into our own hands."

I shrugged. "Fight fire with fire."

"Sometimes you have to fight fire with water. Or with, um, a fire truck. If you don't learn that now, you never will."

I was annoyed, but I wasn't going to take the time to argue with her. "Fine," I finally grunted. "We're obviously not getting anywhere here. Let's go see if Marisol's home. Maybe we can scare *her* into telling the truth." I imagined poor, shy Marisol in an interrogation room with a single lightbulb suspended over her head. Daisy could be the good cop since she was so hot for it. I planned on being the relentless one.

Mrs. Taylor was sound asleep when we got downstairs, so we silently headed out and hit the subway again, this time bound straight downtown.

Marisol's neighborhood couldn't have been more different from Rachel's. Instead of greenery and town houses, the place was a jumbled, jumping morass of power lines, slender apartment buildings, and bodegas. You had to be careful not to get run over by the packs of little kids who were zooming around on bicycles or Razor scooters, and every storefront had a card table out front, with old men sitting around it playing dominoes. I felt my stride opening as Daisy and I headed from the subway exit up the block, feeling the life of the neighborhood pulsing through me. After the too-perfect atmosphere of Dagger Park, this place was a relief.

When we rang up to Marisol's apartment, they didn't even bother asking who was at the door—just buzzed us right in. There was no elevator, so we made the hike up to the fifth floor, where Marisol's mom was waiting with the door open, in a sporty black tank top and tight, casually torn jeans. She had graying blond hair that hung unfettered almost to her butt and a tanned, pretty face, even with no makeup.

"Hey," she said, in a low, friendly voice. "Are you guys friends of Marisol's or something?"

Daisy and I introduced ourselves, and I noticed a flicker of recognition in Marisol's mom's eyes when I mentioned my name. She didn't say anything, though, just let us in and told us to have a seat. I heard a high-pitched whistling noise in the background.

"I was just brewing some tea," Marisol's mom called over her shoulder, heading through the tiny living room into the kitchen. "I hope Oolong's okay."

"Thank goodness it's not cocktail hour here too," Daisy muttered to me under her breath.

"I don't think hippies have cocktails," I whispered.

Marisol's parents were definitely hippies, from the looks of the place. It was covered in dream catchers and Native-American-looking tapestries and hanging plants. There were crystals everywhere. It smelled pleasantly of incense, which, when I looked around, I saw burning on a table in the corner.

Mrs. Bloom emerged from the kitchen carrying a wicker tray bearing four terra-cotta mugs. A solidly built, gray-haired man with a neatly trimmed beard followed. "I'm Sunny and this is my husband, Bruce," she said easily, setting our tea on the coffee table in front of us. "Marisol's just down at the corner getting some groceries. You guys can wait here for her. She should be back in a couple of minutes." The two then disappeared into another room, leaving Daisy and me alone again.

"They're such good hosts," Daisy said. "I wish my mom was that laid-back."

Daisy's mom, Svenska, was the most tightly wound woman I'd ever met in my life. One time, when Daisy had left a pair of underwear on her bedroom floor, Svenska had gotten so mad that she'd ripped it right in half with her bare hands, cursing furiously in Swedish.

"Hippies are always laid-back," I told Daisy. "I actually heard that Marisol was born on a school bus."

"What does that have to do with anything?"

"You know," I told her. "A hippie bus. In the olden days, before all the hippies became public defenders, they used to drive all over the country in school buses and give birth on them and everything. I'm not really sure why. Maybe they liked the color or something. Maybe they longed for the days of elementary school."

Daisy got all bright-eyed at that. "Maybe I should be a hippie when I grow up," she said thoughtfully. "Except I'd like to have my baby on one of those airplanes that has water skis on it and give birth just as we're coming in for a landing in the middle of the Pacific Ocean."

I smiled and shook my head ruefully. "You can't really be a hippie," I said. "You're like thirty years too late. Be something else. Or better yet, just be Daisy. That's more than enough."

Daisy grinned and there was a jangling at the door. When it swung open, we saw Marisol, saddled down with grocery bags. She took one look at me and Daisy sitting on the couch, and her face dropped. As soon as I saw that expression, I was certain that she knew the jig was up.

"Gimme a sec," Marisol said, and went to drop her bags off in the kitchen. When she came back, she just stood in the doorway, arms crossed across her chest.

"What's up, guys?" she finally asked. "Come to start another fight?"

For a second I thought seriously about doing just that, but Daisy placed a warning hand on my knee. The tea had chilled me out a little too, and I decided that it wasn't really Marisol who I had the issue with.

Plus I'd probably get more information out of her if I tried to do things the nice way.

"Marisol," I said with as much sincerity as I could muster, "I'm really sorry about last night. I was just shooting my mouth off. I had no idea what I was talking about."

Marisol softened a little. "I'm sorry too." She sighed. "I told Rachel just to let it go. But you know her. She's too proud to let anything drop. Sorry I didn't stop her."

"I know people like that," Daisy said, for no reason that I could think of. I would have asked her what she meant, but Marisol's words sounded too much like a confession to me.

"So—Rachel *did* take my purse!" I exclaimed.

"Your purse?" Marisol asked, her brow furrowed in confusion. "I was talking about when she spilled that iced coffee on your skirt."

So she had decided to play dumb. Fine. I wasn't going to let up.

"Right," I said, "the iced coffee. Which Rachel spilled so that she could snatch my purse while I was cleaning up!"

"What? No way." Marisol shook her head. "I'd never have let her do *that*. Besides, Rachel may hold a grudge, but she's not a thief."

Now, here's where I wished I had that special girl detective ability to get the truth out of anyone. You know, where they get all steely-eyed and whip out the evidence that makes whoever they're talking to break down and confess all? The problem was, I had no idea what the truth was. I mean, Marisol seemed to be telling the truth. And even if she wasn't, I didn't see how I was going to get her to admit anything that she didn't want to. There was still the possibility that Rachel had taken the purse without telling her friend, but short of catching Rachel red-handed, I didn't know how I was possibly going to prove anything.

Resigned, I got up. "Well, thanks anyway. If you hear anything about my bag, please, please tell me," I begged.

"Of course I will," Marisol said, leading us to the door. As we descended the stairs, she called down after us, "This doesn't mean we're friends, you know!" She laughed, and although she was joking, I detected a note of truth in her voice.

I was still distraught about my loss when we met at Charlie's sister's house that evening. Since Genevieve was technically a grown-up and since Charlie's parents were always out of town anyway, Charlie had been living with Genevieve in a huge nineteenth-century loft in the Brick District—the trendiest neighborhood in town—for the past year and a half. We were gathered there to watch Genevieve's much-heralded television debut.

Genevieve had been plugging away at the acting thing with not much luck for a year. Then a casting director who was friends with her mother finally took pity on her and cast her in a schmaltzy TV movie about the Civil War. Genevieve herself couldn't be there to watch it with us; she was having a big party for the premiere with all her rich girlfriends in some bar uptown, but that was fine with me. Charlie's sister and I tended to butt heads. I could never tell if Genevieve and I really hated each other or if we were just teasing. Probably a little bit of both. I'd known her for so long—since I was born—that I couldn't help feeling a decent amount of affection for her. Even if she was a shallow, supercilious ice princess. Sometimes I got a little nostalgic, in fact, when I remembered how she used to push me down when we played hide-and-seek.

Despite my conflicted feelings about Charlie's sister, I simply couldn't wait to see her movie. Based on the ads that had been running for the past week, it was sure to be terrible, and although Gen's part was too small to make it into the commercial, I knew based on her all-around mediocrity that she was bound to be hilariously bad.

She didn't disappoint.

Genevieve played a slutty Civil War nurse. The fact that they didn't even have girl nurses in those days didn't prevent the producers from decking her out in a low-cut, old-fashioned nurse's uniform and one of those funny hats with the little red crosses on them. Every chance she got, she'd push her arms together across her chest, forcing her boobs together to make them look even bigger. She had the most ridiculous lines to say, too, things like, "That's the most magnificent musket wound I've ever seen, handsome Colonel Francis." She read them like she was reading off the letter chart at the eye doctor's office. About halfway through, when she began a star-crossed romance with a double-amputee Confederate general, I started laughing so hard that I snorted popcorn kernels.

As silly as the movie was, it was kind of cute to see how proud Charlie was of his big sister. He just kept going on and on about how great she had been, recapping all his favorite lines even though we'd just seen the freaking movie.

Why he adores her so much, I'll never understand. I guess it has something to do with the fact that she's his sister and all.

About two hours after it was over, Charlie, Daisy, and I were still lying around on the hardwood floors, tossing popcorn into the air and catching it in our mouths. The conversation had turned back to the stolen purse.

"Nancy Drew and I had a productive day of sleuthing," Daisy told Charlie. "Even if we didn't uncover any clues."

I sat up. "Who, precisely, are you calling Nancy Drew?" I asked, insulted.

Daisy sighed and placed her hand maternally over my own. "Lulu Dark, my little girl detective."

"*Excuse me,*" I proclaimed loudly, "But I am *not* a girl detective. I've read about them, and each one is so worse than the last. They've got no personality, no social lives outside of their obviously gay boyfriends, and absolutely no sense of style."

There was a pause. Then Daisy and Charlie laughed uproariously.

"Well, *excuse* me," Daisy finally said when she had conquered her guffaws. "But you have to admit you were playing the sleuthing game pretty hard. You practically ransacked Rachel's room."

"I did not," I said, wounded. "You can't blame me for wanting my purse back. Girl detectives are prissy busybodies who investigate the disappearance of stolen brooches for old heiresses. I'm just trying to reclaim what's rightfully mine." I shiffed. "Anyone would do the same in my position."

"Oh, sure they would," Daisy said.

"*Nancy!*" Charlie whispered. They erupted into laughter again. All I could do was sit there and watch. Finally, when I couldn't take it anymore, I began pelting them with popcorn kernels.

It didn't help. In fact, it just made them laugh more—until they began retaliating. When a full-blown popcorn fight had erupted, Charlie, the king of gross-out, got the idea to spit the kernels at me instead of throwing them. Daisy quickly followed suit.

I was getting seriously beaten in the popcorn war when Daisy checked her watch. "Crap!" she said. "Svenska is going to kill me. I'm so late." Hurriedly she began to gather up her stuff to leave.

"I should go too," I said, standing.

"Stick around," Charlie said. "It's not even midnight yet. Your dad doesn't care."

"I'm getting kind of sleepy," I said reluctantly. "It's been a long day."

"I'll make some espresso."

I gave in. It *was* still early, and Charlie always knows how to convince me.

So Daisy tripped off to the train, and Charlie busied himself brewing coffee. I hopped up onto the counter next to him and leaned back against the tile wall.

It's funny how comfortable I feel around him. Even though he's, you know, a boy and all and definitely not bad looking, it isn't *that way* with us. He's just Charlie, which is why I didn't feel weird talking to him about Alfy Romero.

"I know he's like way too old for me, but when he was looking at me, at the show, it just felt so *perfect*," I was saying as Charlie handed me a demitasse of espresso. I took a sip. "Perfect," I told him distractedly before going on. "But now it's just like, how do I get in touch with him? I might never see him again as long as I live."

"Maybe it's fate," Charlie said. "Maybe you're not supposed to get together with Alfy."

I rolled my eyes. "If fate didn't want me to get together with Alfy Romero, then why would fate make him give me his number? Fate is stupid. I, for one, don't believe in it."

"I do," Charlie said. He looked at me appraisingly and gave a sheepish half smile. "I think fate, like, makes certain things happen, and then it's up to you to decide how to handle it. You can either play along or you can not."

He turned and made for the living room. I followed him, swigged my coffee back, and lay on the hard floor, arms outstretched like a snow angel.

"So in that case, Charlie, what should I do? I mean, how am I supposed to deal with this situation?"

Charlie lay down next to me on his back with his hand behind his head. "Go with the flow. Chill out a little. Let things happen as they happen. That's what I always do, and everything always turns out fine. Don't worry so much. Just let the world take care of you."

"Whatevs," I said. "That's you, not me. I take things into my own hands."

"Maybe you could learn something from me."

"Likewise." I laughed.

We stopped talking and lay there. The best kind of friend is sometimes the kind you can just enjoy the quiet with. I was just feeling the buzz of the coffee and the steadiness of Charlie's breathing. It was comfortable, you know? Nice.

Of course, Genevieve had to ruin everything by busting in just as I was feeling at my most peaceful. When she saw Charlie and me lying next to each other on the floor, I thought her eyes were about to pop out, even though we were so obviously not doing anything of *that* sort.

I stood up and brushed myself off, trying to maintain a shred of dignity. Genevieve just stood there expectantly, still decked out in her party outfit, tapping her foot expectantly. "Well?" she said finally.

After a beat Charlie took the cue and burst into applause. I quickly followed. Genevieve was loving it, bowing and curtsying and patting herself on the back.

"What do you think? Am I going to win an Emmy?"

"Oh, *definitely*," I told her, and even though I wasn't trying to sound sarcastic, she glared. "I didn't ask you, Lucifer," she said.

"You were great," Charlie said, jumping up and giving her a big bear hug. Genevieve instantly grinned.

"Thanks, little bro. I didn't think I was too shabby either."

I could tell I wasn't going to get away with any ribbing, no matter how gentle, and I wasn't in the mood for another congratulatory retread of the movie, so I began to put on my jacket.

"Where are you off to so suddenly?" Genevieve asked me.

"I promised my dad I'd help him re-lace his shoe collection tonight." I gave her a smirk.

"Well," she said, half grinning, "have fun with that." Then suddenly she had a thought. "But before you go, Lulu, I thought you'd like to know that I saw Berlin Silver walking down the street tonight with a purse identical to that shabby little number you carry. I don't know why she would think it was fashionable; it's obviously a fake and a tacky one, too."

My jaw dropped.

Oh my God! I'd been barking up the wrong tree!

Rachel Buttersworth-Taylor hadn't stolen my purse—Berlin Silver had.

THREE

I WAS LOOKING FORWARD to starting trouble with Berlin on Monday, but when I walked into third-period history, her usual spot in the back of the classroom was empty.

I peered down the hallway in either direction, hoping I'd see her sauntering along lackadaisically or, more likely, leaning against a locker flirting with Jordan Fitzbaum. But she was nowhere to be seen.

I supposed there was a chance that she was just taking her sweet time, but deep down I knew that the girl wasn't going to show. Berlin Silver was nothing but a thieving, spineless chicken.

When class started, I was completely unable to concentrate, although that was nothing new. Today my thoughts were filled with revenge. I was going to make Berlin regret the day her played-out Jimmy Choos ever crossed my path.

I couldn't decide which I was more set on—getting my purse back or showing Berlin Silver who was who. Yes, my purse was important to me. And the phone number, of course. But more than any of that, it was a matter of pride. If Berlin Silver could get away with ripping me off, what was to prevent everyone in Halo City from thinking they could mess with me?

Now Berlin was skipping school to avoid me. What nerve. I ripped a piece of paper from my notebook and dug through my backpack for a ballpoint pen.

THE COWARD! I wrote. I folded the paper into a boomerang and tossed it underhand to Daisy, who had been forced by George, our teacher, to sit three desks in front of me and one diagonal to the left to avoid this very scenario. Daisy and I were too slick for him, though. As my note whipped under desks, spinning a foot above the tile, Daisy swiftly reached under her chair and caught the flying missive, with a barely audible *thwap,* against her opened palm.

George turned from the blackboard. He narrowed his eyes at me suspiciously, but he'd missed the whole thing as usual. He liked to think that he ran a tight ship and that we all loved him because he encouraged us to call him by his first name, but we really thought he was an idiot, due to his obliviousness to the pandemonium that was taking place right under his nose.

It was a constant battle between the class and him, not because we were naturally unruly kids, but because he spent so much time trying to catch us in the act that we just had to respond by living up to his expectations—and thwarting him at every step.

Jordan Fitzbaum was the master at it. One time he managed to write the word *VAGINA* on the blackboard five separate times in one class period without George ever catching him.

George was still motoring on about the Franco-Prussian War when I caught a glimpse of Daisy wiggling her ears. That was my signal. Jauntily I headed to the front of the room to sharpen my pencil, even though I didn't technically have a pencil. George's eagle eyes stayed on me as I passed Daisy's desk, but he was no match at all for that girl, who, with Houdini sleight of hand, invisibly returned the note into my pink cowboy boot.

When I got back to my desk, I unfolded the note and tapped my chin thoughtfully with my pen, which was somewhat battered from the pencil sharpener. *At lunch we'll get Charlie,* Daisy had written. *Take the afternoon off. If we can't get her at school, we'll take the battle to the crook. Fight fire with fire trucks!* I pursed my lips into a satisfied pucker and looked up to see that George was heading in my direction. He had his pointer in hand and a determined march in his step. I smiled at him and shuffled my papers around.

"Your correspondence, please?" George snapped. I sighed with overblown dismay and handed him the decoy that I'd been saving precisely for an occasion such as this one.

"George, it just landed on my desk!" I said, shrugging, "I honestly don't know where it came from."

He unfolded it triumphantly and emitted a high-pitched gasp when he realized that he'd been fooled again.

The decoy was a dog-eared, elaborately folded piece of notepaper that read *VAGINA* in huge black Sharpie letters.

Score.

I'd gotten detention, but that was okay because no one bothered to go to George's detentions. The worst he could do was give you more detention, which you still didn't have to go to. He never bothered alerting the real authorities anymore because he and the head-mistress, Dr. Felicia Bober, were sworn enemies. She'd ignored his pleas for disciplinary assistance ever since October, when he'd melted one of her precious overhead projectors by leaving it on overnight.

Daisy, Charlie, and I met at our usual sunny spot on the terrace for lunch. Then we got to work hatching our plan. Since Berlin had only transferred to Orchard in January, she wasn't in the school directory, but we figured it would be easy enough to find out where she lived from one of her many boy toys.

The first guy we talked to was Adam Wahl, Charlie's friend. We found him in the school parking lot, sitting with his new girlfriend on the hood of his red Saab convertible. Adam was a slack-eyed prep-ster in a tight blue Lacoste polo. He had the collar turned up, of course.

"She lives alone, you know," he told us as his gorgeous girlfriend, Kathy Ramirez, copied his math homework—which he, of course, had copied from Daisy during history. Other than that, Adam had no idea about Berlin's address.

"What else do you know about her?" I asked.

Adam shrugged. "She's gotten kicked out of like ten boarding schools, so her parents decided to send her here to live in Halo City. Orchard was the only private school in the country that would take her."

I was sort of surprised to hear that, really. At school Berlin was mostly just a slacker, not the kind of wild child you need to be to get kicked out. I filed Adam's tip away for later, even if it wasn't going to help me with my immediate problems.

We didn't have much luck after that. We talked to just about everyone else we'd ever seen hanging out with Berlin, and none of them had gotten close enough to her to ever go to her house. It was looking like a lost cause, but I wasn't ready to give up.

Good thing. Because a second later a thought occurred.

"We've been so dumb, you guys," I said to Daisy and Charlie. "Mrs. Salmon has Berlin's address. Let's go get her to cough it up."

We made our way to the main office, where the school secretary, Mrs. Salmon, guarded the entrance to Dr. Felicia Bober's office with zeal. Mrs. Salmon, a pleasant fortyish woman, wasn't mean. But as we quickly discovered, she was completely unmovable.

We pleaded with Mrs. Salmon. We cajoled. Unfortunately, she wasn't about to give up Berlin's address.

Daisy tried turning on the charm. "But Mrs. Salmon," she pleaded sweetly, "I need to send Berlin an invitation to my birthday party!"

Mrs. Salmon gave the three of us a pleasant yet firm smile. "No can do," she chirped, then went back to her task, willing us to leave.

We turned from the office. There were only a few minutes left—lunch period was almost over. If we didn't have Berlin's address by the time the bell rang, we'd have to go back to class.

"Daisy," I said after considering the dilemma for a few minutes.

"Are you still friends with those skaters who hang out in the park across the street?"

Daisy's face lit up. She'd guessed my plan and she liked the sound of it. No surprise there—Daisy always looks best amid chaos.

"Right this way." She turned, walking quickly to the front door of the school. Charlie looked at me quizzically, wondering what Daisy and I were up to. I just gave him a mysterious look. He was going to have to wait and see. We followed Daisy outside, down the front steps of the school, and across the street to the concrete park where all these rowdy skater boys hang out twenty-four-seven.

Daisy marched to the center of the plaza by the big, showy fountain and formed her hands into a megaphone. "Hey, Tripp!" she bellowed. "Come out wherever you are!"

There was a rustling under a bench twenty feet away and a sleepy, wiry skate punk in shredded jeans and a skintight T-shirt emerged from a pile of newspapers. He sidled up to Daisy, hands backward on his hips.

"What's up?"

Daisy leaned in toward him and whispered our plan. Tripp nodded throughout. When it was over, she gave us a thumbs-up and led us back into the school.

"Five minutes," Daisy said, barely able to conceal her giddiness. "We just need to wait outside the door to the office."

After the allotted five minutes of impatient waiting, I heard a low rumbling in the hallway. Slowly it built into a thundering clatter. A red streak flew through the air and Tripp Ratface landed gracefully in front of me.

A second later another wiry skater boy came flying around the corner, then another and another. Before I knew it, the entire hall was jammed with at least fifteen guys on boards, all ollying their hearts out. They bounced off the lockers, turning fancy tricks and stretching their sinewy arms for the fluorescent lights. I burst out laughing. The kids coming out of class just stood there, open-mouthed, staring in amazement.

The door to the office flew open. Mrs. Salmon emerged, carrying a flyswatter like a sword. She chased the punks around the hallway, swatting at them whenever they came close enough. "Out! Out! Out!!" she warbled.

For a second I almost forgot the point of our plan. This scene was too out of control for words. Luckily Daisy grabbed my hand. We slipped into Mrs. Salmon's office, undetected, to grab the file we needed.

Twenty minutes later we were on the subway heading to the Primrose Hotel for Young Ladies, where Berlin's stolen school records claimed she lived. It was strange that Berlin lived in a hotel, but then again, she was a strange girl.

"Daisy," Charlie moaned, the subway vibrating under our feet. "I don't know about this. If I have another unexcused absence, I'm going to lose credit in art."

"Not to sweat," she said breezily. "I'll bring Carla some chocolate."

Daisy was in the killer position of being the student assistant to

Carla Taylor, the attendance secretary at Orchard Academy. Daisy gave her beauty and weight loss tips, and Carla kept trying to set Daisy up with her son Nathaniel, a twenty-three-year-old med student at Halo University. They were like *this*, and Daisy was able to smooth over a liberal amount of class cutting as a result.

We found the Primrose Hotel on the northeast corner of Halo Park. It was a dilapidated, ornate building with gargoyles and gables and everything. Clearly it had seen better days. Still, it was pretty cool.

"I've heard of this place," Charlie said, staring up at the edifice wide-eyed. "My old nanny told me she used to live here when she first got to Halo City."

"I don't get it," I said. "If it's a hotel, why do people live here? And why is it just for young ladies?"

"It's, like, where girls can come and live when they're just getting on their feet," Charlie explained. "There used to be places like it all over the city. The point of them is that they're pretty cheap, but you just get a room, not a whole apartment, and there are all these rules that you have to follow. Like you have a curfew and you're not allowed to have boys in your room. It's some old-fashioned thing."

"Considering how much money Berlin's family has, you would think they'd be able to afford an actual apartment," I mused.

"They must have figured a place like this would encourage her to be less of a troublemaker," Daisy said. "With the curfew and all."

"Nah, my nanny told me that the girls here are always sneaking out and having big parties," Charlie told us. "You know how those young ladies can be." He gave Daisy a wry look.

The proprietor of the Primrose was a stocky woman in an oversized hockey jersey with a short, gunmetal gray hairdo. Her name, according to her name tag, was Mel.

"No boys allowed!" she barked at us when we walked in. She was sitting behind a big oak desk with one of those little reception bells at her fingers. She banged on it a couple of times for emphasis, a jittery *ding ding ding*. "This is a home for young ladies!"

"Oh, Charlie's not coming upstairs," I said, crossing my fingers behind my back. "We just want to ask you a few questions."

"Well, ask away," Mel responded jovially. She tapped the bell a few more times before she folded her arms behind her head and leaned back in her chair. "I know everything about this place and the girls living in it, too."

As she spoke, I noticed a buff guy in just his boxers sneaking out of the elevator behind her. He slowly tiptoed behind a big potted palm, where he stood, stick straight, trying to blend in with the leaves. Mel didn't seem to notice.

"I'm looking for a tenant named Berlin Silver," I said, trying to ignore the half-naked interloper.

Mel nodded knowingly. "Yep, yep, Berlin Silver. Quite a gal. With looks like that, she should be one of them models or something or a whatchamacallit. An actress."

"I need to see her," I said.

"She's in school. Least she better be. Nope, you can't go up."

"So she lives upstairs?" Daisy asked. It was the dumbest question ever, but miraculously, it worked.

"Of course she lives upstairs," Mel said in a patronizing voice. "You're on the ground floor right now. She lives in 3C. I gave her that room so she could study——her being a student and all. Now, if I'd given her anywhere on the fifth floor, that would have been a problem. Them girls up there think they're rap musicians and so forth." She shook her head ruefully.

"Always making a racket, those fifth-floor girls. I don't call that music myself. Me, I call it noise. I said to those girls, I said, 'Ladies, I know a thing or two about music, and if Celine Dion couldn't sing it, it's not very musical, now, is it?'"

As she sat there, lost in thought, the naked guy emerged from the potted palm and went streaking out the door of the hotel, making an expert getaway. I could see that Mel had a lot in common with George the history teacher. Daisy and I knew just how to play her. Finally she opened her eyes again.

"Where are your friends?" She seemed confused.

I turned to my left and found myself as befuddled as she was. Daisy and Charlie had disappeared.

"Maybe they went to the bathroom?" I bluffed.

"Oh. Okay. Well, that puts me in mind of a story. I remember this one time that . . ."

Oh no, I thought. *Does it never end?*

But before Mel could get into her story, there was a clatter from behind her. She swung around. Three girls looked up with panicked faces that said BUSTED. Between them they were trying to roll a keg of beer from one elevator to the next. I gave them a sarcastic thumbs-up. Good job, guys!

You could tell it pained Mel to have to interrupt her story, but keg parties were obviously against the rules of the Primrose Hotel.

"Amanda! Charlene?! *Elizabeth Prives!?* What's going on here?" Mel demanded.

I wanted to stick around for the scene, but I had a feeling that I knew where Daisy and Charlie had gone. I needed to find them.

Taking a chance that the heavy swinging door next to the entrance led to a stairwell, I snuck toward it at full tiptoe speed while Mel confronted the girls.

"But Ms. Raymond! We were just practicing for the big barrel-rolling competition next week!" I heard a shrill, whiny voice protesting as I pulled open the door.

Bingo! Stairs.

No time to eavesdrop. Letting my stealth drop, I raced up the steps two at a time. The stairwell smelled like a foul combination of gym clothes, Victoria's Secret body-spritzer, and nail-polish remover.

When I got to the third floor, I was out of breath.

At the top of the flight Daisy stood next to the door, back pressed against the wall. She put a finger to her lips. "Charlie's trying to get into Berlin's room," she whispered. "You should help him—I'm going to stand watch here."

I nodded and swung open the hall door. Charlie stood in the hall, hunched over the doorknob to room 3C, busily fiddling.

"What are you doing?"

He looked up at me like I was an idiot. "Picking the lock, duh." He clutched a subway fare card, which he slipped smoothly into the crack between the door and the door frame.

"Since when do you know how to pick locks?"

"I don't, but I've seen them do it on TV a bunch. Plus this looks like a really cheap lock."

I wanted to help him, but Charlie was too busy showing off to accept any assistance. He fumbled, trying to press the lock back with the flimsy fare card. All it did was hang flaccidly in the door crevice.

"Maybe if you watched more TV, you'd be better at it," I teased. He shot me a withering glance.

At that moment Daisy's head came popping around the hall door. "Hide!" she whispered urgently, then disappeared.

Charlie grabbed me by the waist and, in one motion, pulled me into the broom closet directly across the hall.

Those two had some nerve accusing *me* of being a wannabe sleuth. Charlie and Daisy were the ones who were acting like this was some big mission: impossible.

There were muffled voices in the hall. I couldn't tell what was going on, but I felt reasonably confident that Daisy would be able to handle whatever Mel threw at her. Charlie, on the other hand, was a different story. He couldn't talk his way out of a brown paper bag. If he was caught up here, we were dead meat.

I was so busy straining to hear Daisy that I barely noticed the fact that Charlie was still clutching me around the waist. My face was about *this close* to his neck, and he smelled like a funny combination of laundry detergent and milk. I know that sounds gross, but there was something comforting about the smell. We were both breathing quickly, nervous that we were about to be discovered. When I paid close attention, I almost thought I could feel his heart, thumping nervously in his skinny rib cage.

Suddenly there was a rattle at the doorknob.

It was Mel, and she was about two seconds from discovering us. "Never seen so much beer on the floor in my life," she was telling Daisy. "Well, maybe back in seventy-nine, when I was bartending at Annie Oakley's. But that's another story. Man, I never did like those sixth-floor girls. Think they play by different rules. Now I gotta mop up their mess."

The doorknob was still jiggling. "Dang," Mel huffed. "This door is always jamming. Now, if I could just get one decent repairman in this place . . ."

Charlie pulled me tighter, and even in the dark I was afraid he could see me blushing.

Please, Daisy, I thought. *Work your magic. And hurry!*

"You're going to mop up *their* beer?" Wonderful, loyal, true Daisy's voice sounded. "Don't you think that since they threw the party, they should clean up the mess themselves?"

A long silence. I held my breath.

"Sweet cakes," Mel finally said, "you've got a point there. Gotta teach them kids a little respect." I could hear footsteps and the voices receding.

The sound of the swinging stairwell door echoed through the hall outside, and I exhaled heavily in relief.

"Close call," Charlie whispered. His face was unexpectedly near to mine. I could feel his eyelashes on my cheekbones and his slow breath on my face. A small tingle went up the back of my neck and a strange thought entered my head.

Charlie was about to kiss me.

If I'd been thinking rationally, I would have backed away, or turned my face, or *something.* But I didn't—I guess I was in shock or something because I just stood there and closed my eyes, waiting for his lips to touch mine.

Thank goodness Daisy swung open the door just in time.

Me and Charlie? Please. My life was complicated enough. The adrenaline pumping through my veins must have induced some form of temporary insanity.

When the light from the hall came bursting into the broom closet, I jumped about a mile in the air and then realized that for the third or fourth time that day, I had been rescued by perfect timing.

Daisy didn't seem to notice the fact that Charlie and I were in a somewhat intimate position. "I'm brilliant!" she congratulated herself. "Now let's break into Berlin's room."

I quickly composed myself and stepped out of the closet. "Charlie was having a hard time with the door," I said with, I guess, a hint of snark.

"Can't I leave you two in charge of anything?" Daisy asked. She stepped toward Berlin's door and pulled a bobby pin from her back pocket. She poked it gracefully into the keyhole. With a thoughtful expression and a never-mind flick of her wrist, she coaxed a satisfying *pop* from the bolt. "What a cheap lock," she said.

Charlie was annoyed. "Where did you learn how to do that?"

"There's this magical box in my living room that, like, makes pictures that move? It's called television. Maybe you've heard of it?"

"You're going to have to teach me that trick," I told her.

"You'll need it if you're going to be a famous girl detective," she said.

I decided not to dignify her comment with a response.

Inside, Berlin's bedroom looked like it had just been demolished by a mob of angry *Jerry Springer* guests. The drawers had been flung open. There were clothes all over the floor. The bedsheets and blankets had been ripped off the bed and strewn all over the room. At the sad little wooden desk in the corner, a sad little wooden chair had been flung on its back with the dead and gory aspect of roadkill or unsold purses at the end of a sample sale.

"What a pig," Charlie said. "You'd never guess it from looking at her, would you? This is practically as filthy as my room."

"No, it's not," Daisy and I said, almost in unison.

"Your room is full of dirty dishes and half-eaten food, and you never bothered to sweep up that wastebasket you knocked over a month ago," I reminded him.

He frowned. "I was going to sweep it up tomorrow," he said. "And what if I want to eat some of that food later? It's still good, you know."

The thing is, Berlin's room really wasn't like Charlie's room at all. Aside from the clothes and sheets and general disarray, there wasn't much in it. I couldn't imagine that this was how Berlin really lived. Girls like her may be messy, but their mess usually involves lots of fashion magazines.

"There's something weird about this room," I said, taking the opportunity to reapply my lip gloss.

"Yeah. It's like she has no personality at all," Daisy said. "There are no decorations or anything."

"True, but that's not what I mean. I can't quite put my finger on it." Then a thought occurred to me. "You know, it looks like Theo's apartment . . . after it got broken into!"

Theo is my dad's scandalously thirty-ish boyfriend. His apartment was burgled about a year ago, when he, Dad, and I were on vacation at the beach. All the robbers took was his really old, very smelly baseball card collection, which didn't seem like that big of a deal to anyone except Theo himself, who claimed (unconvincingly) that the cards were priceless.

The thieves had totally ransacked the place, though, looking for the more valuable stuff that didn't exist. After the robbery his place had looked a lot like Berlin's room—drawers flung open, everything strewn around randomly. . . .

"I think Berlin's been robbed," I declared.

"How do you know that?" Daisy asked.

"It's her *intuition*," Charlie sniped. "All amateur sleuths have it."

Charlie was really getting a kick out of tormenting me. Boys can be such jerks.

"Shut up," I said. "I'm totally right. Look how everything's been scattered all over. Someone was looking for something."

"I think it's just a mess," Daisy said carefully. "Your purse has got to be in here somewhere. It might take a few minutes to find it. Let's just cross our fingers that Berlin doesn't come home."

"I hope she does," I said. "She deserves what she gets when she steals someone's favorite handbag. I'd like to tell her where to stick it."

Daisy rifled through some of the clothes on the floor. "Just as long as you don't end up needing a ride to the hospital."

I snorted. "If anyone's going to the hospital, it's *her*."

Charlie and I quickly got to work panning through the detritus in search of my missing bag. I was holding my breath, hoping to see the telltale beaded fabric, the hot pink strap.

"She's got more clothes than even Genevieve," Charlie said, practically buried in a pile.

"Yeah, and what's the point when they're all totally the same?" I mused. "I mean, who really needs ten sparkle tube tops in different shades of blue? Who even needs *one* sparkle tube top, for that matter?"

Suddenly I spied a swatch of hot pink under a pile of crap in the corner of the room. I lunged for it, triumphant. My beloved purse!

But as I grabbed at the fabric, I realized, with a sinking feeling, that it lacked the satisfying, familiar heft of my handbag. I lifted it from the pile. It wasn't a purse at all. It was a crumpled, hot pink pair of underpants.

Yuck! I tossed them at Charlie, and he recoiled clumsily, not sure how to react.

We stayed at it for what seemed like forever, and after discovering about five hundred pairs of crumpled-up underpants, we realized that the purse was straight up not there. Charlie and Daisy thought I was silly for insisting that the place had been robbed, but I still thought I was right. In the back of my head I couldn't help worrying that someone had stolen my purse from the original thief—Berlin.

We were just about to leave when Daisy chirped with surprise from the corner by the dresser.

"Hello! What is *this?*"

She held up one of those jewel-studded nameplate necklaces that everyone was wearing like two years ago.

"Ha!" I exclaimed. "Berlin would never wear that now. It must be a gift from the Ghost of Bad Fashion Trends Past."

"I don't think this is Berlin's," Daisy replied. "Look." She tossed it to me from across the room. When I examined it, I realized that she was dead right: it couldn't be the heiress's. For one thing, I quickly saw that the jewels on it were plastic. Berlin is all diamonds all the time. But more important was the fact that instead of spelling out Berlin's name, the letters on the necklace spelled out a mysterious, lonely word: *HATTIE.*

I stared hard at those six sparkling letters and then, holding the necklace up to my throat, I examined my refection in Berlin's mirror. There was no doubt about it: this was evidence. The real question was, how had gotten into Berlin's room? I gave the trinket one last look before slipping it into my pocket, and then we were off.

FOUR

THE BEST THING ABOUT JUNIOR

and senior year at Orchard Academy is the third Friday of every month, which the powers that be like to call "Future Career Day."

I guess the idea, once upon a time, was that the older kids would get a day off to research what they're going to be when they grow up. Like, to follow some lawyer around for the day or help a doctor perform surgery.

Of course, now everyone uses the day off to sleep late, catch up on *Days of Our Lives*, and eat ice cream for breakfast. Then you have to write a paper about it, saying what you did and how it supposedly will help you gain job experience. The trick is making it sound like you actually did something without technically lying.

Eventually Dr. Felicia Bober, the headmistress, banned food taster and TV critic as acceptable future careers unless you spent the day hanging out at Nabisco or *Entertainment Weekly* or something, but we all found a way around that rule pretty quickly.

For our part, on this particular Future Career Day, Daisy, Charlie, and I were being more productive than most, using the time to continue our pursuit of Berlin Silver. She hadn't shown up in school all week, and I was getting itchy to find her. I hated to say it, but the case of the pilfered handbag had become a full-fledged mystery—especially since we'd discovered the state of Berlin's apartment.

Despite my most charming efforts, none of the administrators at school would give me any clue as to her whereabouts. So we decided to stage a stakeout. Figuring that Berlin would have to be coming and going at some point, Daisy and I set up camp in the park across the street from the hotel, hoping to catch her in the act.

I'd brought my digital camera along because truthfully, I do want to be a photographer when I grow up. I figured I'd just snap a few pictures and pass it off as "career" research. Daisy, on the other hand, claims to want to be a synchronized swimmer. There was no way hanging out in Halo Park was going to help her with that—unless she decided to do her hanging out in the fountain.

Instead she decided to change her career goal to investigative reporter. It wasn't as glamorous as synchronized swimmer, but she was relieved not to have to wear a swimming cap. (Although I know she secretly thinks the swimming cap is sort of cool.)

Charlie had passed on spending the day with us. His grandmother had given him a boatload of cash to buy a new wardrobe, under the condition that he let Genevieve pick out all of his clothes for him. Charlie, of course, was humiliated, but he wasn't about to turn down the money. And Genevieve was thrilled—like a little girl who has just gotten a very fancy doll to play with. Charlie was disappointed not to be able to come with us, but he swore up and down that he would ask about Berlin at every boutique he visited.

It wasn't that much of a stretch—with the kind of clothing addiction that Berlin's room revealed, she was bound to have been seen by one of the shop owners recently.

"How on earth are you going to turn a shopping spree into a Career Day paper?" I asked Charlie when he told me his plan.

"My future career is rich dilettante," he explained.

I rolled my eyes. Charlie just couldn't stop screwing with authority. "Such a rebel," I said. "Let's just hope it doesn't turn out to be the truth. Your sister's already chosen that career."

"No. She's an *actress,*" he'd told me testily. "And at least I'm being honest. Unlike, you know, everyone else." He paused. "It's not like I wouldn't rather be with you anyway, Lulu. As much as I love Gen, this dress-up thing is going to be a nightmare."

"True," I agreed.

Daisy and I had work to do, but I couldn't help feeling bad for Charlie. With Genevi*evil* picking the outfits, he was probably going to end up looking like a very large poodle. And he was missing out on a fun day of spying.

For our rations I brought thermoses of coffee and gourmet pastries that my dad got from the deli down the street. Daisy supplied the blanket, sunblock, and a transistor radio.

I mean, if I was forced into this girl detective game, at least I was going to get a tan in the process. Spring was at its most beautiful, and I needed to get nice and bronze before summer. Plus we'd be more undercover if we were lying on a blanket.

All in all, it was a pretty sweet setup. We picked a perfect sunny spot on the grass directly across the street from the Primrose Hotel for Young Ladies. We laid down our blanket, stripped to our bikini tops and shorts, and started watching.

On our stomachs to start, facing the entrance to the hotel, we waited. And waited. And waited. The only people who left the hotel were three boys and a really skinny girl carrying a corgi in a basket. No one went in. It seemed like we'd been watching the door for an eternity or more when the egg timer went off.

"Fifteen minutes," Daisy said. "Time to flip."

I turned dutifully onto my back and realized that all I could spy on from this position were clouds.

"Daisy, we're never going to catch her like this," I complained.

"Well, we can't get half a tan, can we?" Daisy asked rhetorically.

I sighed. "I just wish she'd show already."

"Relax, Lulu," Daisy soothed. "You don't get a good tan if you can't sit still for at least for twenty minutes."

"Hello!" I said, exasperated. "This is about getting my bag back, remember? Besides." I sat up and gestured. "There are all these hot guys just wandering around *totally unattended,* and we're ignoring them."

Daisy perked up. I knew that would get her attention.

My hope was that we could hit on some new information while hitting on some*one.* Or better yet, several ones.

Based on the principle that the people most likely to have information on Berlin were the type with a Y chromosome and based also on the fact that the park was teeming with ultra-choice specimens thereof, I hatched a plan.

It went like this: when we spotted a guy we wanted to talk to, we went up to him, still in our tanning outfits, and explained about Future Career Day. I'd snap a digital photo, and Daisy would conduct a brief investigative interview on the Berlin question. It seemed like the perfect way to kill not two but three birds with one stone.

Working decidedly on our side was the fact that Daisy was in her bikini.

Don't get me wrong. I'm happy with what I've got, but Daisy's boobs are practically too perfect to even exist. For some reason, they make guys act like they've been sedated.

Berlin and Daisy must possess a similar kind of magic when it comes to the male of the species because we quickly encountered three guys who were all pretty familiar with the missing Miss Silver. None of them had seen her recently, though, and they weren't that interested in talking about it anyway. They were too busy drooling and staring at Daisy. She didn't seem to notice.

There was Joshua, a writer for the *Halo Reader,* who was dressed down in expensive-looking jeans and a white T-shirt. He had dated Berlin in January before realizing that she was seventeen, not to mention slightly weird. Those were his words, not mine. Personally, I would have described her as *way* weird or possibly even *a total mutant.*

Then there was Lars, a dreamboat house DJ from Germany who had dated Berlin in March. "Her name, you see," he told us in adorably broken English. "It reminds me, yes, of my home, and she is quite lovely, too. But she has many secrets that she not speak. I think maybe, such as, she is not honest about I'm not sure, you know?"

I certainly *did* know, but it hadn't done me any good yet.

I thought about offering Lars my number, but when I took out my notebook to scribble it down, he entered into a deep conversation with Daisy. Something about "the perfect beat." I didn't want to bother them, so I decided to be nonchalant. I opened my camera and snapped a picture of the fountain instead.

The guy who seemed to have been closest to Berlin was Marcus, a deeply bronzed out-of-work model. When Daisy asked Marcus about Berlin, he got a faraway look in his eyes.

Actually, I was afraid for a second that he was going to cry, which would have been way too embarrassing for me to handle. He told us that he had fallen head over heels in love with Berlin in February, only to have her drop off the face of the planet after he'd told her that he wanted her to meet his mother.

The weird thing was that however smitten, not one of these guys seemed to know any real details about Berlin, outside of how gorgeous they thought she was.

I was trying hard to resist, but it was difficult not to feel a little sorry for Berlin. She was certainly popular, in her own ignominious way, but no one seemed to really *know* her, not by a long shot. It was kind of sad.

Even Marcus, who still seemed beat up over the fact that she had ditched him, was really surprised to learn that she lived right across the street.

At the last minute, dangerously close to sympathy, I put on the brakes and reminded myself that if Berlin the thief was cut off from people, it was no one's fault but her own. One way or another, her relationships with all these guys had ended because she hadn't been willing to show them who she really was.

Daisy must have been thinking along the same lines because once Marcus had shuffled off, her sensitive side came out with a vengeance. "Poor Berlin," she said. "She must have been so lonely."

"I thought you were the one who hated her most."

"Well, she does bug me, but you have to wonder why she shuts everyone out. Practically all those guys would have totally fallen for her—if she had let them."

Anxious for some Berlin news on any front, I called Charlie on his cell.

"No luck yet," he told me when he answered, his voice staticky on the other end of the line.

"None here either, hombre," I reported.

Inexplicably, he added, "Not a chance."

"What?" I asked.

"There is no way I'm wearing a dickey. I don't care who the designer is." I realized that he wasn't talking to me, but to his sister.

"Charlie!" I snapped.

He came back to earth. "What?"

"How many places have you checked?" I let a hint of irritation creep into my voice.

"Well, just one, but . . ." He paused. "Genevieve's been torturing me all morning. You should see some of the stuff she made me buy. On second thought, you never will because it's going straight to the back of my closet."

"Charlie, you've only checked *one* place? Are you interested in helping or are you interested in buying a new wardrobe?"

"Lulu," he said peevishly. "Don't blame me. This wasn't my idea. And may I remind you that it's not my stupid purse."

Charlie was right. This was my fight. Not his.

"Well, you'd better watch it, buddy," I teased. "I can always get another sidekick. Batman has replaced Robin like three times, you know."

"Four if you take *Crisis on Infinite Earths* into account," Charlie said. "But anyway, who says you're not *my* sidekick?"

"Ha!" I said. "In your dreams, pal."

"Listen," he said. "I've gotta go. I have to stop Genevieve before she buys me a five-hundred-dollar beret. I'll join you guys as soon as I can."

I said goodbye and clicked off the cell. I smoothed on a new coat of lip gloss, thinking. Something was up with Charlie, but I couldn't quite place my finger on it. I hoped it didn't have anything to do with the broom closet episode.

I spaced out for a moment, considering the possibilities, each one of which was more troublesome than the last. When I looked back up at Daisy, she was freaking out—gesturing frantically and craning her neck in about five different directions. Was this her attempt at the hula?

"Lulu! Lulu," she said urgently, "turn around!" Aha. This was her take on subtlety.

I spun and scanned the park. Across the grass, walking the cutest little bulldog I'd ever seen, was the one and only lead singer of the Many Handsomes. It was Alfy Romoro.

He was looking as good as ever, in a tight red T-shirt and shredded blue jeans hanging cool and low on his perfect butt. Alfy's dog hovered adorably around his ankles, dangling a Frisbee from his slobbery jaws.

My head was spinning, overloading on hotness. Daisy could see that I was about to be hopelessly crushed out. "Stay cool, Lulu," she warned.

Too late. I was off like a shot.

The boy and his dog had already turned in the opposite direction and were marching along at a steady clip. Good thing Alfy chose a fat little bulldog for his pet or I might have lost him. As it was, I made a mental note to take up jogging with Daisy again.

"Stay cool, Lulu," I repeated to myself.

I didn't want Alfy to think that I was some overeager freak, even if it was somewhat true. And it was hard not to look at least a little desperate when I was sprinting after him like my life depended on it.

I finally caught up with him while his dog was peeing on the concrete path. I took a sec to smooth my hair and quickly press my glossy lips together. Then I called after him from behind.

"Alfy!"

He turned, leash in hand, and gave me the blankest look ever.

"It's me," I said, with an awkward, twitchy little half wave. He didn't say anything. Why wasn't he as overjoyed to see me?

"Remember?" I reminded him, stepping closer. "We, um, we met at Big Blonde the other night? And you said I should call you but . . ." I laughed nervously. "There were these two girls, see, Marisol and Rachel, and they totally hate me and everything, and Rachel totally spilled her coffee on purpose and then this total jerk named Berlin? When I got back, my purse was gone! So that's why I haven't called."

Alfy stared at me like I was a lunatic.

My hand sprang up to cover my mouth. My brain had obviously melted down and my body was taking over, telling me to *shut up, shut up, shut up.* Nothing I had said had made any sense at all. I wanted to clarify, but I knew that if I tried to say anything else, it would come out in pig Latin.

Alfy furrowed his eyebrows in confusion. "Sorry," he said. "I think you have the wrong guy."

"No! Alfy Romero! That's you, right?" Thank goodness for small favors. My English had returned. Not that it seemed to make any difference.

Alfy nodded slowly, still unsure.

"I was at the edge of the stage and you gave me your number right after the encore. Well, *you* didn't, but . . . Remember?"

"No," he said. I thought I saw a look of bewildered recognition in his dopey puppy eyes, but maybe it was just wishful thinking. We just stared at each other. The dog was sniffing around my feet, but I ignored it.

"Sorry," Alfy finally said. "That never happened." He gave the leash a jerk. "C'mon, Pumpkin." His bulldog perked up, at attention, and Alfy hurried off with Pumpkin trotting behind him.

"But . . ." I called out. It was too late, though. I was completely humiliated.

I sat down against a huge tree, trying to make myself as tiny as possible. If I thought about it hard enough, I hoped, maybe I could become a blade of grass.

Guys. They were the problem, not me. They're so weird and fickle. It's like, they're all desperate to get with you, but as soon as you act like you might actually be interested, they treat you like some insane, pathetic Ophelia type who's going to send them pig's hearts as Valentine's Day presents. Well. Alfy Romero certainly didn't know the first thing about Lulu Dark. I'm about as likely to go fatal attraction on him as I am to become best friends with Berlin Silver. I'm an *empowered* woman.

Besides, if he didn't want to go out with me, he should have just said so. True, I would have probably punched him in the face, but hey, he would have deserved it.

I couldn't help but wonder: how many random girls did he bestow his number upon, only to forget after a week? And for that matter, how could anyone forget a girl like me? Even if he only saw me in pitch darkness, I like to think that I'm pretty unforgettable.

Still, sprawled out against that tree, I tried to find the bright side. Perhaps no one had witnessed my little encounter. When I looked over at Daisy, I found her frolicking in the fountain with a bike messenger and a golden retriever. Well, that was something.

Unfortunately, upon a look in the other direction, I felt that spark you get when you meet eyes with someone by accident.

About fifty feet away the girl we'd dubbed Sally Hansen was filing her nails. Except she wasn't looking at her hands. She was staring straight at me—with total and utter hate in her eyes—just like the other night.

What was with this girl? Did she have some problem with the state of my cuticles or something? I reached for the camera around my neck and, quick as a fox, I snapped her picture. Ha! That would show her to conduct her personal grooming in public.

Sally jumped, startled. Then she turned and shuffled off in her black miniskirt and stilettos. The girl was a pro, too: not many people can walk that fast in high heels.

I considered chasing after her to ask what her problem was, but I was still winded, not to mention discouraged, from my pursuit of Alfy.

Anyway, what was the point? What could I possibly say to her besides, "Stop giving me mean looks while you do your nails"?

No, I didn't confront Sally. Instead I resigned myself to the fact that this had been the worst Future Career Day ever. We'd come no closer to finding Berlin *or* my purse, I'd been dissed hard core by the world's cutest boy, and meanwhile my best friend was about to win the Miss Halo Park pageant. I hadn't even gotten a tan—just a nasty sunburn on my shoulders and nose.

Enough was enough. I decided I deserved the night off.

FIVE AFTER THE DEBACLE IN THE PARK

Charlie met me and Daisy at Little Edie's, where Daisy is the most absentminded waitress of all time. When Charlie arrived, it was five o'clock, and the place was totally empty. Daisy turned the music way up and poured us all some coffee.

Little Edie's is on the corner of Conford and Culp avenues, in the so-called funky part of town, where sixteen-year-old punks clog the sidewalks. It's the best place in the world to hang out, especially when Daisy's working. When it's empty, we have the run of the place, sitting on top of tables and walking around with our shoes off, and when it's full, it's crowded with the biggest oddballs in Halo City. The furniture all comes from thrift stores and yard sales—basically junk—so it looks like someone's weird bachelor uncle's apartment, with huge, comfy armchairs all loose springs and stuffing popping out in a thousand directions. There's a black cat named Big Edie who wanders back and forth, purring and rubbing up on your leg and expecting anchovies in exchange for affection. At Little Edie's, Daisy gives us free food and lets us stay forever at the table by the window, just watching people and having bizarre conversations with strangers. During the summers I practically live there.

That day, even though the hour was inching toward evening, the sun was only just beginning to turn pink on the edge of the window frame. I plopped myself onto a busted BarcaLounger, and Daisy and Charlie shared the antique divan.

"I think today may have been the worst day of my life," I told them.

"Aren't you overlooking the occasion when you peed your pants on the fourth-grade field trip to the zoo?" Daisy asked. Charlie laughed.

"Ugh, don't remind me." I covered my face with my hands. "Maybe it's a tie."

"Lulu, you're always so dramatic," Charlie said. "Think about how much worse it could be. Someone could have died. Your hair could have fallen out overnight. You could have broken a leg or worse. In the grand scheme of things, one jerky boy isn't all that bad."

"Charlie, it wasn't just a jerky boy. I made a complete fool out of myself."

Daisy stood and walked over to the counter, where she began wrapping up silverware in napkins for the evening crowd. "Actually, Lulu," she called, "I'm not sure about that. If he thought you were hot a week ago, why shouldn't he now? It's not like you grew a second head or something. If anyone should feel disgraced, it's him, not you."

"Yeah. And besides, you can do better," Charlie added.

I looked at him quizzically. "You think?" I asked.

"You *know*," Daisy interjected, "something strange is going on. I mean, what's up with that Sally Hansen girl? What was she doing, stalking you?"

I sighed. "I don't know."

Charlie drummed his fingers on the table and tapped his foot to the flamenco music that Daisy had put on the sound system. He has the shortest attention span, and he was getting bored with the conversation.

"So what's the plan for tonight, Lu?" he asked. "How are you going to find Berlin now?"

"I'm taking the night off," I told him. "This is totally not working, and I'm exhausted from thinking too hard. I feel like I'm missing something. Maybe if I chill on it, the solution will come to me."

"As long as you're not giving up," Daisy said.

I looked at her incredulously. "Hello, this is Lulu Dark you're talking to. Winners never quit and quitters never win. And at this point I'm mostly just in it to beat Berlin at her game. It's not like I'm going to call Alfy now that he thinks I'm a freak—so the issue of his number is pretty moot."

"You could give it to Genevieve," Charlie suggested. "She keeps talking about how jealous she is."

I set my coffee mug on the table with a loud thump. "Charlie," I said slowly, "if you tell Genevi*evil* what happened with Alfy Romero today, I will *kill* you. I don't need her and her little minions laughing at me all over town. If Genevieve is jealous, I would prefer it if she stayed that way."

"I won't say a word. But if we're not searching for Berlin tonight, what *are* we doing?"

"Whatever it is, count me out," Daisy said. "I'm working till two in the morning."

"I just want to take it easy," I told Charlie. "I don't think I have the spirit for anything too exciting. I've been hammered down by life." I sighed loudly and sank into my seat, playing for sympathy.

"I have just the place to go," Charlie said. He smiled broadly and brushed his hair from his eyes.

A couple of hours later we were sitting at one of the best tables at Medardo, which is maybe the trendiest restaurant in Halo City. Charlie's dad, who is a pretty famous lawyer, totally adores me, and when Charlie told him I'd had a terrible day, he gave him the credit card and told him to take me out. It's like impossible to get a reservation at this place, but Charlie's family has all the right connections. The lights were dim and there were candles flickering everywhere. I was looking good, if I do say so myself. I'd changed into this slinky, electric blue dress that one of my crackpot mom's fashion designer friends had given to me last time I visited her in LA. I paired it with my hot pink cowboy boots. I missed my purse a little——it would have matched so well——but even without it, I was looking fine. Charlie wasn't too bad himself. As a joke, he'd donned his Gucci suit for the occasion and, more shockingly, a vintage floral tie. He'd even smeared some junk in his hair, which he never, ever did.

When we approached the table, Charlie jumped ahead of me and pulled out my chair.

"Your seat, Ms. Dark," he said in his lowest baritone.

"Why, thank you, Mr. Reed," I replied, slipping into my seat. I grabbed my menu and a hunk of bread. I sat there for a moment, munching and trying to decipher the contents of the menu. It was puzzling. Is a sweetbread like a doughnut? I was pondering the question when Charlie looked up at me. "We look hot tonight," he said, smiling out of one side of his mouth. "I mean, we look good together. I mean"—he blushed—"I like your dress. Never mind."

"Why, thank you, Charles," I said, batting my eyelashes playfully. "I think you just said something very charming."

A relieved look came over his face. I held his gaze for a moment, but before it got too serious, we both erupted into laughter.

As we were recovering, a waiter placed a plate of something complimentary in front of us. I examined it. It was hard to tell exactly what it was, but it appeared to be some sort of shellfish with sherbet on top. That seemed weird to me, but you never can tell when it comes to this fancy business.

"We'll have a bottle of wine too," Charlie said to the waiter as he was about to walk away.

"Would you like to see the list?"

"We'll just take whatever's nicest," Charlie said. "Red."

My eyes almost popped out of my head. "He means whatever's *cheapest*," I jumped in. It was a nice gesture, but I wasn't about to drink a five-thousand-dollar bottle of wine on Charlie's dad's tab.

The waiter could barely conceal his smirk but nodded anyway. "I'll pick something for you," he said. We didn't even get carded. Eating out with a guy who knows the owner certainly has its advantages.

I had to restrain myself from tipping my chair back to get a good look around the restaurant. It was dim and noisy and elbow to elbow with people, and I had to lean in close to Charlie to hear him over the warm buzz of laughter and the smooth, pulsing bossa nova that hovered in the air. I craned my neck to take in the crowd and was almost positive that I saw several supermodels in different corners, all picking nervously at salads. I sighed happily as I felt an easing of the tension that had been sitting in my shoulders all day. Charlie was right. This was exactly what I needed.

When our food arrived, we'd each already had a couple of glasses of wine. I'm not sure what it's like to be drunk, and I don't think I was, but I do know that I was feeling a little sillier than usual, tossing my hair a lot and fluttering my hands around when I talked, which I was doing a mile a minute. Charlie seemed to be in the same mood, his eyes wide with amazement at everything I said and his limbs suddenly very limber. After our entrees we both fell back lazily into our chairs. I'd been spacing out for several minutes, involuntarily thinking about my purse and Berlin and Alfy Romero, when I glanced up at Charlie again and saw him busily constructing an intricate little structure out of sugar cubes in the empty spot where his plate had been.

That was Charlie for you. Always acting grown up but deep down, the same little kid I'd known my whole life. I laughed to myself, but he picked up on it.

"What's so funny?" he asked.

"What are you doing with those sugar cubes?"

"I dunno." He shrugged. Then he smiled and looked me straight in the eye. "I'm going to reconstruct the Great Pyramids. For you. I might need to ask the waiter for some more sugar cubes, though."

"You're such a spaz," I said, kicking him under the table. But I was secretly touched. The Great Pyramids. I liked the sound of that. I felt my heart swell a little but caught it just in time and shook it off.

Anyone who saw us probably would have thought we were boyfriend and girlfriend. Luckily I knew better.

The thing is, Charlie is cute, like, *really* cute. He's all tall and starry-eyed and full of action. But I could never date him—I know him way too well. And I know his flaws better than probably anyone in the universe. Like what a dilettante he is, and how spoiled and oblivious. And how he cracks his knuckles *constantly*, and bites his nails, and is never ever on time. He's also a total flirt and is way too fickle with his girlfriends. Seriously. He'd been through five or six already that semester. It's like, he tries them out for a while and when they don't measure up to some crazy ideal he has in his scruffy little head, he dumps them.

Anyway, as I said, Charlie and I would never, ever work.

"Look," he said, pointing across the room and not even trying to be subtle. "Jordan Fitzbaum is hooking up with Rachel Buttersworth-Taylor!"

"You're kidding," I said, and swiveled to see. He was only exaggerating a little: Jordan and Rachel were there, on an obvious date. I noted with satisfaction that not only did they have the table by the kitchen, but their outfits weren't anywhere near as stylish as ours.

Nonetheless, Rachel had definitely scored a coup. She'd had a huge crush on Jordan since eighth grade, and she'd finally gotten him to take her out—to Medardo, no less. Jordan *was* gorgeous, too, practically underwear-model material.

"God, I hope she doesn't see me," I said. "That's the only thing that could make this day suck worse."

"A piano could fall on our heads while we're walking down the street," Charlie said. "That would suck worse. Or I could spill wine all over your one-of-a-kind frock." He picked up the bottle and playfully taunted me, tipping it in my direction.

"Don't!" I exclaimed. "Don't even joke!"

He put the bottle back on the table. "See," he said, "it could be much worse. What could little old Rachel do to you, anyway?"

"Well, *she* could spill wine on my dress. Somehow that doesn't seem out of character for her."

"True story." Charlie was silent for a minute, smirking.

"What are you giving me that look for?"

"I don't know, I just think it's really funny how you and Rachel hate each other."

"Why shouldn't we?" I snapped.

"Because you two are just like each other. You could be sisters. Or soul mates." Charlie grinned smugly and crossed his arms across his chest as if to say, *Take that.*

I was floored. How could Charlie possibly think I was anything like that insecure, vindictive witch? "What! Do! You! Mean by *that?!*" I demanded.

"Put it this way," he said with that annoying look of triumphant satisfaction. "You're both incredibly smart and cool."

I scowled.

"And you're both totally tough. You can call Rachel what you want, but she's no wimp. You both know what you want and how to get it. It's just that neither of you can stand that there's someone else around like yourself. You each want to be the only one. So you should get over it and just be friends."

"You are so wrong!" I protested.

"Lulu, I'm so right. Everyone knows it except the two of you. Marisol and I talk about it all the time."

"You talk to *Marisol?*"

"Only when I know you're not looking. She's actually really nice."

"This is too much," I said. "I'm leaving."

In a huff, I began to gather my things. But Charlie took my hand from across the table and held it tight.

"Don't leave," he said. "For one thing, there's still dessert."

I thought about it. The pastry chef at Medardo *had* won all these big awards. His desserts were supposedly the most delicious you could get in the world.

"Fine," I finally said. "But you better take back what you said."

"I'm not going to," Charlie told me. "Anyway, if you had been paying any attention, you would have noticed that I just gave you like five killer compliments. You just get so caught up in your little wars that you can't see straight sometimes."

"Untrue!"

"True! So do everyone a favor. Just think about it."

I leaned back in my seat, capitulating. It was a fact that I was trying to turn over a new leaf—be a little nicer and less prone to jumping to conclusions—I guess that was the goal. And I had already been wrong about Rachel a few times in the last week. Maybe she deserved one more chance. But if I ended up with another dead fish in my backpack, there was going to be hell to pay.

For dessert I got this chocolate-and-raspberry thing that looked like the Leaning Tower of Pisa, and Charlie ordered a soufflé that was served on fire. When it came to the table, the flames from his plate were shooting up over our heads, low Brazilian music was weaving through the air, and everything suddenly seemed very romantic again. Charlie was glowing orangey in the mellow light. I noticed the tiny scar on his chin and suddenly remembered how he'd gotten it, back when we were in third grade together.

It had been my fault. I've always been a daredevil and Charlie— well, in those days, at least, he was sort of a scaredy-cat, not to mention obsessed with following the rules to the precise letter. I was always showing off, doing the stuff that everyone else was too chicken to even think about, and every day I'd try to top myself, attempting a stunt even more outrageous and against the rules than the day before. On the day that Charlie got his scar, I'd finally worked up the nerve to tackle the one thing that even I'd been afraid of.

The jungle gym on the playground at the lower school of Orchard Academy isn't actually that tall. But when you're eight years old, things look more impressive than they really are. In third grade, let me tell you, that jungle gym appeared truly unconquerable, the tallest thing ever erected for climbing. It had been built back in the fifties, when kids were *expected* to do crazy stuff and no one worried about safety concerns, so the thing was metal and complicated and treacherous. Nowadays, if you tried to build something like that, you'd have some group of Concerned Mothers Against Fun on your back in a second, petitioning city hall to ban playgrounds altogether for the safety of dim toddlers.

No kid that I knew of had ever climbed to the very top of that jungle gym, which was shaped like a big cylinder of twisted iron. Mostly everyone just hung around under it, pretending it was a clubhouse or digging pits in the wood chips in the hopes of finding a worm to chase someone around with. Every now and then some boring girl would climb a couple of rungs up and hang upside down, but even that activity stopped when Rachel Buttersworth-Taylor pointed out that they were allowing the entire world to see their underpants.

I for one have rarely cared if anyone sees my underpants. It's not like they're dirty or anything, so big deal. That day on the playground, I decided that I was going to conquer the jungle gym no matter what. So I climbed and climbed and climbed while all the other kids just stood around staring. Every time I glanced down at Charlie, far below, he looked like he was about to have a heart attack, red-faced and bug-eyed, fists clenched tight.

Like I said, Charlie used to be a little neurotic.

When I got to the terrifying crossbar that ran across the tip-top of the jungle gym, I heard him call out after me.

"Come down, Lulu!" he yelled, in that panicky, whiny screech he had before his voice changed. But I didn't pay attention. Instead I used my arms to hoist myself onto the narrow metal beam, standing straight up with a grand flourish. There was a collective gasp from the crowd below and then Charlie's voice again. "Lulu! Stop!"

Heedless, I placed one foot in front of the other, hands outstretched like a tightrope walker, and slowly made my way, one foot in front of the next, to the very middle of the structure, twenty feet off the ground and nothing but spiky wood chips to catch me if I stumbled. When I reached the sweet spot in the center, I dropped to a crouch and grabbed the bar, using momentum to swing my knees over it so I could dangle, upside down, in the place where no one had ever dared to dangle.

Triumph!

I had been hanging there for about a minute, congratulating myself on my own bravery, when I started to really feel the blood rush to my head. It was time to come down.

And then a terrible thought dawned on me. I had no idea how to reverse my position. The way I was dangling, I couldn't manage to swing my arms back up to the bar. I was stuck.

I kept hanging there, wondering what I could possibly do. My head was really aching, and the kids below were whispering frantically. They could all see the predicament that I was in. The only way out was to drop. It wasn't actually *that* far, I decided, and maybe I would break a leg and get to wear a cast, which might be a novelty. Then I felt a cool breeze on my butt. My skirt was hanging around my neck. Maybe it was all the blood in my brain, but for the first and only time ever, I was embarrassed about the fact that everyone could see my underwear. I had to get down from there if it was the last thing I did.

I flexed my legs, trying desperately to straighten them enough that my knees would release their grip and send me plummeting to the ground. It wasn't much of a solution, but it was something.

Ironically enough, as I was dangling there in the air and praying to fall, gravity was working against me. Suspended I would stay.

There was really nothing left to do. If it hadn't been beet red because of my unfortunate position already, I'm sure my face would have flushed like never before. Humiliated, I heard a pathetic, tinny squeak creep from my throat. "Help!" I peeped.

There was some conference on the ground. I couldn't really see or hear what was going on, but after a moment I saw a figure ascending the jungle gym.

"I'm coming, Lulu!" Charlie warbled. His shout sounded weak and unsure.

It felt like he took forever to reach me. I started to wonder if I was going to pass out. Eventually there was a shadow in the corner of my eye. From what I could tell, Charlie was creeping, on his hands and knees, across the beam to the point where I was suspended.

When he reached me, his voice, along with the rest of him, was trembling. "Grab my hand," he said, and reached for me. When I felt our fingers touch, I wheezed with relief. Shakily he yanked and pulled my hand up, giving me just enough of a head start to reach the beam.

At that point it was no problem for me to lift myself back up, but as I did it, Charlie wobbled.

"Uh-oh," he croaked.

And then, as if in slow motion, he was falling, in skydiver pose. I was perched safely at the top of the jungle gym, and I saw Charlie hit the ground with an ominous thud. When he rolled over, there was blood on his face.

In the end, he'd been lucky. He'd been stabbed in the jaw with a sharp wood chip, but otherwise he was all right. I got in big trouble for being such a show-off, and he's had the mark, about half an inch long, ever since.

Scarred for life, all because of me.

I guess he could have been mad at me about it. But instead, we became inseparable.

Charlie was never the same after that, and honestly, it was kind of a good thing. From that day on, all his nervousness, all his striving goody-goody ethos simply evaporated. There was hardly anything that made him nervous anymore.

With that in mind, eating my fabulous dessert at Medardo, I decided that whether I forgave Rachel or not, I forgave Charlie for comparing me to her. If he was criticizing me now, it was only because he had my best interests at heart.

When my mom left, seven years ago, Charlie was the only one who noticed how truly upset I was. Only Charlie could cheer me up because he was the only one who had any idea that there was cheering up to be done. A year later, when I was freaking out because my *dad* had taken up with a *man,* Charlie was there to tell me it was no big deal.

So, long story short, Charlie's the greatest and like I said before, he's extremely good-looking.

I shocked myself by thinking, *What if we* were *out on a date . . . ?*

I rolled the idea over in my head, watching Charlie devour his dessert. Scooping up bites in that endearing, messy-boy way, dropping a little on his lapel, wiping it off and licking his fingers. Here he had gone to all this trouble, making a reservation, getting dressed up (which he never does), ordering wine, dessert, everything.

"Want a bite?" Charlie said, offering me his spoon.

Whoa, I thought. *What if he thinks this is a date?*

"No, thank you," I said as graciously as possible. I knew I'd have to let him down easy.

There's something a little sick about dating someone you've known since you were practically in baby carriages. Something almost like *incest,* right? You can't get much grosser than that. Maybe having a torrid romance with a hamster or a goldfish is worse, but that's pretty much the only thing I can think of, and I surely didn't want to commit any crimes against nature. No, it simply could never be.

Charlie was scraping the final bits of soufflé from the dish when he spoke. "By the way, Lulu," he said uneasily, "I hope you don't think this is a date or something."

I practically choked on my water. I smiled, making a quick recovery. "Why would I think it was?"

"It's just that, you know, I didn't want you to get weirded out or something. Thinking that I was all liking you like that. Because I totally don't. I mean, you're my best friend. But I'm not trying to make it something that it isn't. I just wanted to, you know, have a nice dinner in fancy clothes. And make you feel better."

I felt a knot forming in my stomach. How could I have been so dumb?

"Charlie," I said, trying to stay composed. "I know the difference between a date and two friends having a good time. Don't worry about it. I'd never want to date you."

Charlie smiled, tight-lipped. "Good. Because, you know, I wouldn't either. Want to date you, I mean. Of course not."

"Well, it's settled, then," I told him.

We waited for the check in silence. I couldn't figure it out. I was actually disappointed. And pissed off. I decided that I probably had a mental problem. I would have to talk to my doctor about this. Maybe there was some kind of medication that would make me less of a freak.

As we were getting up to leave, I told Charlie to hang on for a second. Even if he didn't think I was girlfriend material, I'd decided that he was right about Rachel, at least the part about not being a bitch to her. There was no point in having enemies. The one exception was Berlin Silver. She would be my enemy *for life.*

So I walked over to the table where Rachel and Jordan were sitting. I was hovering over Rachel's shoulder, waiting for a pause in the conversation, when Jordan looked up and saw me.

"Lulu Dark," he said. "What's up? We saw Charlie's flaming dessert. Very impressive."

"Yeah, pretty awesome," Rachel said sarcastically.

I turned to her. She didn't seem pleased at all to see me, and I took a deep breath, bracing myself to eat crow. "Look," I said. "I just wanted to let you know that I'm sorry about what happened the other night. And everything in general. It's stupid for us to hate each other, so let's just bury the hatchet. My friends all say you're cool, so why not, right?"

She wasn't buying it. "Lulu Dark," she said, "you are a total hypocrite. Forget the other night. What about the fact that you've been spreading gossip about me all over town? You think I don't know what's what?"

She lowered her voice and continued. "You know, it's really messed up, even for you, telling everyone that I have a third nipple."

"What?" I yelped, shocked. "I didn't tell anyone anything about you!"

It was true. I hadn't said a word about Rachel to anyone except

Daisy and Charlie. And I *definitely* didn't tell anyone anything about a third nipple.

"Save it, Lulu," Rachel said, dismissing me with a wave of her hand. She picked up her fork and turned back to Jordan, adding sweetly, "Just for the record, I have the appropriate number of every single body part. Two eyes, two ears, ten toes, et cetera."

Jordan's jaw dropped, and he looked like he was about to heave. I wanted to get out of there before Rachel attempted to prove her case, so I scurried off, turning only to see Jordan waving a furtive goodbye with a desperate *rescue me!* look on his face.

This was why it didn't pay to be nice to Rachel. It always backfired. I'd probably show up at school on Monday to have her pull some vicious prank on me again. I shuddered to think what it would be.

But I wondered, why would she make something like that up? Just to have an excuse to be mean to me? That made no sense. If she thought she was impressing Jordan Fitzbaum that way, she was wrong, too—dead wrong. He looked ready to bolt at any minute. So what in the world was Rachel thinking?

Things were almost back to normal after Charlie and I left the restaurant. Even if my attempt at conciliation was a failure, he was proud of me for it. As for the rest of what had happened, it had been really narcissistic and unfair of me to assume that Charlie was into me. I decided to put the idea out of my mind for good.

"So what's the plan now?" Charlie asked as we wandered up the bustling street, being spare-changed left and right by kids who prob-ably live in mansions when they're not busy playing homeless. Charlie bounced on the toes of his Pumas and reached his arms for the moon. "Are you ready to go out?"

"Not really," I said. "But Dad and Theo want us to come by for poker. The girls from the softball team backed out."

"Sounds good to me," Charlie said. "I'll win big."

We headed off to my place.

Dad and Theo are totally different from anyone in Charlie's family, and I think he's a little jealous. His parents and grandparents and aunts and uncles and sister and even her dog are all variations on the same theme: the most stuck-up, anal-retentive beings in the universe.

Every now and then I think Charlie even wishes he had parents like mine. And that includes my mom, because she's allegedly such a "free spirit." Personally, I think "free spirit" is just a nice way of say-ing *irresponsible lunatic,* but whatever. She's fun to hang out with when she's in town.

My mom and dad got divorced when I was five, but mom didn't move away until I was almost ten. I guess she left because she freaked when Dad started dating Theo, but still, she could have considered her only daughter before moving all the way across the country.

The thing is, even when she was supposedly "around," she hardly paid any attention to me—except when she needed a child as an accessory, like to pose with for *People* magazine profiles.

My mom's name is Isabelle Dark, and she used to be slightly famous. Now she's pretty much a has-been, although sometimes people still recognize her on the street from her most famous movie, *Sorority Vampire Party*. In that movie she played the president of an evil, bloodsucking sorority that preys on drunk frat boys and turns them into zombie slaves.

Nowadays she plays, like, sassy judges, mean social workers, and Julia Roberts's neurotic mom. And that's when she works at all.

Mom's always been insane, which according to my dad is why he liked her in the first place. He says it's also what makes her a good actress.

Lucky for me she lives on another coast, because I don't think I'd be able to cope with all of her issues. That responsibility falls on the shoulders of the endless parade of beefcake models that she dates—and more power to them.

While I'd been thinking about Isabelle, Charlie and I had made it back to my neighborhood, where my dad has lived since he was a twenty-two-year-old starving artist. Our street used to be all factories and warehouses, and I guess back in the day it was considered pretty sketchy. But over the years a bunch of artists moved in and turned the warehouses into really cool places to live. Lucky for Dad—he got in when it was really cheap, and now it's pretty much the best place to live in Halo City.

Since Mom moved out, it's just been me and Dad, which is the way I like it. I never bothered to ask Dad what his deal was—why he married a lady and then got with a guy. It seems like his business, not mine, and everyone is happy with the arrangement at this point. Sometimes Theo talks about moving in with us, but I don't think it will ever happen. He lives only a few blocks away, and he spends so much time at our place anyway that it seems pointless to go to the trouble of making it all official.

When Charlie and I entered the apartment, Dad and Theo were chilling in sweatpants, with the stereo pumping and popcorn popping in the microwave.

"You kids ready to get your butts kicked?" Theo asked. "I've been reading up on strategy since last time."

Yeah, right, I thought.

Every single time we play poker, I take everyone for all they're worth. They're always saying they're going to beat me, and it never happens. You should see my bluff: it's unstoppable.

"You guys look fancy," my dad said. "How was your date?"

"It wasn't a date!" I yelled, without meaning to.

"Jeez. Sorry," Dad said. He was trying to look very serious, but he had a smile in his eyes. "I had no idea. All I know is that when someone takes me someplace like Medardo and dresses up in his fanciest Gucci suit, it's a date."

"I don't even *have* a Gucci suit," Theo pointed out, piling on. "I'm strictly a Men's Warehouse kind of guy."

Charlie looked like he wanted to turn around and run for the hills. He's not used to having my dad make fun of him. It tends to be the three of them against me.

"Charlie and I are just friends," I told Dad and Theo judiciously. "You guys should know that by now. After almost *seventeen entire years*."

"Thank you for reminding us," my father said. "You guys just look so good together that it's easy to forget."

Charlie's face had turned a sick shade of green. "Let's just play," I said, mustering all of my magnanimity.

We all sat down at the card table, gearing up. I put on my customary poker visor and began shuffling the cards, pulling a few flashy moves to intimidate everyone.

"No way," Theo said. "We are not letting that card shark deal anymore. She cheats. She has some trick."

Sometimes Theo can be such a baby. I looked to Charlie for support, but he just put out his hand. "I'll deal," he said.

"Whatever, you guys," I told them. "You'll see who's laughing when I win again."

"In your dreams, Lulu," Theo challenged. "My new strategy is unbeatable."

As I raked in the chips like always, I told Dad and Theo about my terrible afternoon. I left out all the Berlin Silver stuff because I didn't think Dad would approve of my sneakiness and I didn't want him to do something embarrassing like call the headmistress and demand to have Berlin suspended.

"And then," I was saying, "he pretended not to know me! He acted like a complete stranger!"

Dad and Theo were both laughing, which I didn't appreciate.

"He told me I must be looking for some *other* Alfy Romero! As if!" I said indignantly, trying to bring the point home. They weren't having it at all.

"It's *not funny!*" I finally yelped, when it became clear that they had totally missed the point of the story.

"I'm sorry, Lu," Dad said. "It will seem funny in a few months' time, trust me."

"It will not! It will always be humiliating. When I'm old and withered like you guys, it will still be humiliating."

"Who are you calling old and withered?" Theo said. "I'm only thirty-one."

"Exactly," I snapped.

"Whatever," Theo said. "You're too boy crazy, Lulu. It's clouding your judgment."

"You should have seen her at that concert," Charlie said. "Every time he glanced anywhere near her direction, it looked like she was about to pass out. Like a starstruck eight-year-old at an *NSync show."

"That's my girl," Dad said. "Lulu has always been very passionate. Just like her mother."

I shot them both my patented Lulu Dark death stare. One eye for each of them. Sometimes being the only girl in a room full of guys can be a trying experience. They have, like, no respect.

"You people are such hypocrites. Especially *you,* Theo," I said. "You have some nerve calling *me* boy crazy. I've watched those *ER* reruns on cable with you. I see how you swoon over George Clooney. Anyone who thinks George Clooney is sexy has got to be *old*. He's at least sixty himself!"

The only good thing to come out of the argument was that it seemed to be taking everyone's mind off the poker game. Everyone except me, that is. I laid my cards triumphantly on the table to reveal that I had a truly golden hand.

The guys sighed as I pulled another pile of change to my corner, cackling.

"I told you she cheats," Theo complained. "She has some trick involving mirrors and rubber bands."

"Lulu's sneaky," Charlie said. He smirked. "You don't even know the half of it."

"Well, no worries. This is all part of my strategy," Theo said. "I'm going to make a comeback in the second half."

He didn't, though. In fact, he was the most hopeless player out of everyone: the type who would play a pair of twos as if it was a full house, raising and raising, expecting me to fold under his bluff. Unfortunately for him, Charlie was right when he said that thing to Berlin the night that my purse was stolen. Not only can I see through walls, I can also see through crappy bluffs. So we kept on playing and I kept on winning. No one was really that grumpy about it. They had gotten used to it, and for all their bluster, they accepted my superior skills.

In the end, I bankrupted everyone. I let out a whoop and immediately began counting the spoils of my victory, loudly proclaiming each dollar.

"Give it a rest, Lulu," Theo finally said. "You can count your riches later. Not that I know what you're going to do with a big pile of nickels: you need a quarter to even buy a gumball in this day and age."

"It's legal tender," I gloated. "I'm going to roll them up and take them to the bank. I've got at least ten bucks here."

He didn't pay me any mind, though. "Hey," he said brightly, bare feet on the coffee table. "I forgot to tell you guys about the brilliant inspiration I got this morning."

I can't quite tell you what Theo does, but I know that he's pretty successful—borderline famous, in fact, like my dad. He sort of writes plays, except that he doesn't call them that. Every time you ask what he's working on, he gives you some crazy new answer that makes no sense, like that he's working on a one-man avant-garde electro-musical. He always talks in hyphens like that, which is totally silly but endearing.

"Oh yeah," my dad said. "Tell them about your new play."

"It's not a play," Theo corrected him predictably. "It's more like an experimental neo-drag cabaret performance piece. It's going to be called *I Was a Teenage Shark Witch*."

Charlie wrinkled his forehead. You could see he had no clue what Theo was talking about.

"So in other words, it's a play," I clarified.

Theo gave me an exasperated look. "I *suppose* you could call it that—if you insist. Anyway, it's about a girl who's half shark and half teenager. Kind of like an evil mermaid who likes to go to the mall. Oh yeah, and she's dead."

"Tell them where you got the idea," Dad said eagerly. Clearly he thought Theo's idea was totally brilliant—which I didn't understand. Then again, Theo's ideas always sound dopey when he talks about them. Then he goes ahead and wins a Pulitzer or something, so you never can tell.

"From the newspaper this morning," Theo said. "There was this article about a body that they just found in Dagger Bay. A teenage girl. She was dressed to the nines in designer clothes. And here's the cool part—she had a tattoo of a silver shark on her hip bone. And it's like, why a silver shark? Why was she in the bay? Who was the girl? Why did someone want to murder her? And . . ."

Theo was going on and on, but I wasn't listening. The room was spinning and I was afraid I was going to throw up. Unless I was hallucinating, things were a whole, *whole* lot worse than one stolen purse.

Why? Because Berlin Silver had that exact same tattoo—right on her hip bone. No one had seen her in a week. *And* her apartment had been ransacked!

My brain was throbbing, as if it had just expanded to twice its normal size. A murder had taken place. There was no way around it. Berlin Silver had been *murdered!*

I didn't want to worry Dad by telling him—he probably would never let me leave the house again if he knew that one of my classmates had been offed. But Charlie had to be thinking the same thing as me, and I needed to figure out what to do. This was just too much for me to handle alone.

"I need to get something from my room," I said, abruptly standing up. I signaled to Charlie to follow me, but he already knew what I was thinking. He followed with a haunted look on his face while Dad and Theo just looked on, bewildered.

"Are you okay, honey?" my father asked.

"I'm fine," I croaked.

"I guess the lovebirds are retreating to their nest," Dad teased.

Theo rolled his eyes. "Leave them alone," he said with a snort. "I've heard that teenage girls need some privacy now and then."

We reached my room and I slammed the door, barricading us inside.

"Okay, I'm completely freaking," I wheezed.

"Don't freak," Charlie said at precisely the same moment.

"How can you say that!? Berlin Silver has been brutally murdered, and you tell me not to freak out? What is wrong with you?"

"Whoa, whoa, slow down," Charlie said. "I know it's a weird coincidence, but there's no reason to think Berlin has been murdered."

"Charlie, how can you be in such denial? They found Berlin in the bay this morning."

"No," he said calmly. "They found a woman with a shark tattoo. There's a difference."

"But—it has to be her. How many people have that exact tattoo in that exact same place?"

"Probably a lot," Charlie replied. He's very good at coming up with explanations that have no other purpose than to make him feel secure about the world. "Think about how many people have Tweety

Bird tattoos. Or Betty Boop. Or 'I Heart Mom.' I think you're jumping to conclusions. Trust me."

He put his hands on my shoulders, trying to keep me calm, but it wasn't working at all. His explanation was straight up not plausible.

"Charlie," I said, "that's the dumbest thing I've ever heard. It's *got* to be her. She's been missing for a week, her room was trashed, *as if by a criminal*, and the dead girl has the exact same tattoo."

Suddenly another thought occurred to me. "And my purse!" I gasped. "Charlie, someone murdered Berlin and now they have my purse, with my ID in it and everything!"

"Lulu, get a grip. I bet you anything that Berlin is at school on Monday. With your purse, which she'll return. And then you can kiss and make up—not that you would ever do that. Anyway, you'll see. Everything is going to be fine."

My head was throbbing. I could tell that I really *was* about to get a migraine. "It's not fine!" I wailed. "We have to do something right now!"

"Lulu, come on, what can you possibly do? Let's just rent a movie and chill, okay?"

"A movie?" I gasped. "You've got to be kidding me."

Charlie gave me his hurt puppy dog eyes. "Maybe you'd feel better if we just went out for a little bit," he said hopefully. "Big Blonde is still open."

"Charlie, I'd rather French-kiss Regis Philbin than go to Big Blonde at this moment." I was completely pissed off that he was being so cavalier. "If you wanted to go out tonight, why didn't you go on a date with someone you were actually interested in?"

Charlie looked wounded. He didn't say anything—just turned around, opened the door, and slunk out of the room. I felt bad, but really, it was something that needed to be said.

I was a mess. Worse, Charlie was right. There was nothing that I could do right now. I stripped off my dress and collapsed into bed.

It took me forever to fall asleep. I tried doing the meditation exercise that Dad taught me to conquer insomnia, but it was no use. I was tossing and turning, thinking about Berlin. True, I never really liked her, but she didn't deserve to be murdered. And then there was the thing with my purse. Whoever killed Berlin could be coming for me next. It would be so easy, with my name and address and even my picture inside. I knew, without a doubt, that my life was in danger.

Then it occurred to me that perhaps I was being self-centered. A person had been murdered, and all I could think about was my precious Korean purse and what was going to happen to *me*. Suddenly I felt sheepish. My self-absorption had gone too far. *Maybe I should take up the Kabbalah,* I thought. It seemed to work for Madonna—although not so much for Britney Spears.

When I finally settled into sleep, it was no escape. In the dream I had, I was at Oscar's, the fanciest department store in all of Halo City. Now, going to Oscar's is always a stressful experience because of the persnickety shopgirls and horrible, pushy customers trying to steal your size and butt in line, and in my nightmare all that was blown out of proportion. I could feel everything in the store, the walls and racks of expensive clothes, closing in on me, and I was positive that someone was chasing after me. So I ran into the dressing rooms.

For some reason, I wasn't wearing shoes, but I had my purse again. It didn't make me feel any better.

I fled from my pursuer through mirror after mirror, each one swallowing me like water and spitting me out into another identical dressing room. I could feel someone following right behind me, but every time I looked over my shoulder, I saw only my own reflection, smiling monstrously. And then the fire alarm went off, a beeping that started soft and became louder and louder until it was screaming in my ears.

I woke with a start, sweaty and breathless. The department store had evaporated, and I was in the blackness of my bedroom again. But the beeping had gotten louder than ever. It was coming from my bedside table.

My cell phone was ringing, I realized. Groggily I reached over and grabbed it. UNKNOWN CALLER, the display read.

"Hello?" I mumbled, picking up.

"Hi!" The voice on the other end was cheery. It actually sounded quite a bit like my own voice.

Was my mom calling? It would be just like her to forget the time difference and ring me up at three in the morning.

"Who is this?" I asked, still half asleep.

"This is Lulu Dark," the voice went on. "Listen, I've lost my phone, and I guess you found it. Have there been any messages for me?"

I groaned. Someone was playing a joke, and this was definitely not the time for it.

"Who is this?" I demanded. "Who is this *really?*"

"Um, hello? I told you already, this is *Lulu Dark.* Personally, what I want to know is who *you* are, besides a thieving little fink."

I gasped. Was this person serious? She certainly sounded it.

The stranger gave a long, peeved sigh before she continued. "Here's the thing: if you don't return my cell phone, you'll be sorry. So make it snappy."

Then, before I could ask any more questions, she'd hung up.

SIX

I WOKE UP THE NEXT MORNING WITH the vague feeling that something was wrong—something that I couldn't put a finger on. *I must have had a bad dream,* I thought, *the kind that ruins your day even though you can never quite remember it.* But when I rolled over and saw my cell phone lying on my pillow, it all came flooding back—the shark girl, the creepy phone call.

None of it had been a dream, as much as I would have loved to think otherwise. Berlin Silver was dead, and no one knew about it but me.

The more I thought about it, the more I was convinced of what I had to do: I had to head straight to the police station, tell them about Berlin, and hopefully come home with a full retinue of uniformed protection—in case the murderer was coming after me next.

I dressed quickly and hit the door. On the walk to the station Halo City felt more sinister than ever before. Every corner seemed sharp with potential danger. I jumped at each little noise, knowing that Berlin's murderer was somewhere on these streets and knew everything about me—including my cell phone number.

Too bad I'd always laughed at Daisy for her karate lessons. If I were a brown belt like her, I wouldn't feel like such a wimp.

My feet carried me toward the station as fast as they could.

Keep moving, I told myself. *Just a few more blocks to go.*

I made a quick turn onto Laight Street—and stopped short.

Sally Hansen was standing on the other side of the road—at the traffic light—waiting to cross the street. Despite the heavy flow of traffic between us, she locked eyes with me. She stared at me with a menacing glare.

My heart skipped a beat. This was the third time I'd run into her. Was she following me?

The look on her face told me I'd better wait till I had Daisy's backup to find out what was the deal.

I spun around and hightailed it out of there before the light changed. I ducked around the nearest corner and, once I was certain that I was a safe distance away, slowed down enough to whip out my pocket notebook.

I scribbled the words *SALLY HANSEN!!* and the date on the first blank page, then hastily shoved the notebook into the back pocket of my jeans.

So what if I'd started keeping a notebook? Plenty of people do it; it has nothing to do with being a detective.

I picked up my pace again and decided on an alternate route to the police station. I practically sprinted there, looking over my shoulder the whole way. Luckily I didn't see Sally again.

I didn't expect the police to take me seriously. I expected them to roll their eyes and run me off, saying something like, "Listen here, chippie. Why don't you leave the detective work to the professionals?" And as such, I prepared myself for a fight.

But unlike everything you see in cop shows and read in mystery novels, the police didn't turn me away immediately. In fact, they seemed very interested in what I had to say.

The detective I spoke with was a tall, heavily made-up woman named Detective Wanda Knight. She and I got along right off the bat. She respected me the instant I complimented her on her lipstick— which I recognized as MAC Berry Lip Blush, applied, of course, with a brush.

"Oh, you're good," she told me, smiling. "You have excellent powers of observation. You might make a good detective yourself."

I cringed, but she didn't take any notice.

"Now tell me what you know about the tattooed girl," she said. "All we've got so far are a couple of dead leads. Maybe you're the break in the case we need."

I told her everything I'd said to Charlie the night before and was gratified when she took my information seriously, unlike some friends I might mention.

"It's certainly an unusual tattoo," she said thoughtfully. "And in silver. I didn't even know there was such a thing as a silver tattoo until this case. But you say she disappeared just last week?"

"That's right." I nodded. "The last time I saw her was on Friday."

"Well, it can't be the same girl, then. The body we found has been in the bay for at least four months."

I was exasperated. Why do the police always get so caught up in the tiny little details? *Hello,* big picture! If this is the way that law enforcement operates, it's no wonder they still haven't found Tupac's killer.

"Listen, Detective Knight," I said firmly. "Maybe some of the pieces don't go together, but I'm positive that the girl in the bay is Berlin Silver herself."

The policewoman squinted at me. "What makes you so sure?" she asked.

I was caught off guard. I'm not used to being doubted. I was sure the body was Berlin because I had a hunch—and my hunches are always right. But I obviously couldn't say that unless I wanted to sound like a total bimbo.

"Well . . . I—I don't know!" I sputtered. "It's just obvious! Isn't it?"

Detective Knight seemed to suppress a smirk. "Listen, Lulu." She patted me on the back. "I can tell you one hundred percent for sure that the dead girl is not your friend. There's just no chance. That body we pulled from the river has been in the water for so long she's got no—well, let's just say it's not pretty. As for the tattoo—it's not much, but I guess it's something. I'll look into it—and I'll see if I can dig up something on this Berlin Silver character, too."

"If you figure out where she is, can you call me?" I asked.

The woman raised one eyebrow. "Are you the new district attorney?" she asked dryly.

I scowled.

"Sorry," the detective said. "I couldn't resist. I saw them say that on *Law and Order* once."

Seeing the disappointed look on my face, she gave an understanding smile. "Thanks for your help, though. I promise that everything will be fine. I'll do my job if you do yours: stay in school and just say no to drugs, street gangs, and underage drinking."

I just looked at her.

"Kidding!" the detective said. "I'm trying to cheer you up. Have a sense of humor."

I was glad to know she cared, but frankly, I didn't think it was a time for joking around.

I was dejected when I left the office. My meeting had gone nowhere. And despite what Detective Knight told me, I still had no doubt that Berlin was dead.

Perhaps I was being irrational, but it didn't matter. It was easier to accept the idea that the laws of nature had gone screwy than the idea that I could somehow be wrong.

After my street-side run-in with scary Sally Hansen, I decided it would be safer to take the train to my next stop, the DMV. I boarded the blue train where I always do—second car from the back—and searched for a seat. As I walked toward the front of the car, I heard the sound of a familiar voice. I turned and discovered that the

Teener (known to teachers as Christina Schmidt) was aboard the train with her posse of anonymous cronies.

The Teener's crew are Orchard Academy's resident stoners. I've always gotten along fine with them, even if they are incredibly boring. All they ever do is smoke a bowl, watch cartoons, eat some Bugles, then smoke another bowl and watch more cartoons, of course. They all have the sallow-faced look of shut-ins, which is basically what they are. I wonder if they pee in bedpans.

It was strange to see them out on the subway on a Saturday afternoon. Normally the only time you catch them outside school is at three in the morning—in the D Street Diner—gorging on chicken fingers and pizza fries. They keep to themselves, though, and don't normally bother anyone, so when I spotted them, I wandered over to say hi.

I didn't think anything was out of the ordinary when the Teener and her gang began giggling at my approach. That's the status quo with them: they're all in a constant state of giggle.

"Hey, Teener," I told the group with a nod. "Hey, everyone."

They all broke into giggles again, and it took a good minute before they calmed down enough for the Teener to talk.

"Hey, Lulu," she finally said. "We were just talking about you."

I recoiled. I didn't know that this crew ever talked about *any-thing*, much less me. I thought they just napped and giggled and threw potato chips at each other.

"All good things, I hope," I said evenly.

"We heard you've been hanging out with Margot and Millie Stratford."

"You heard *what?*" I asked incredulously.

Margot and Millie Stratford were the most notoriously detestable twin sisters in Halo City. They were like Genevieve and Berlin Silver combined and magnified by a trillion. Their great-grandfather had founded a cigarette empire, and now they were unbelievably rich. I'd run into them on a few, unfortunate occasions, at parties at Charlie and Genevieve's, and they were even worse than the gossip pages made them out to be. They spent their days getting their beauty rest in the penthouse of a sixty-story high-rise (probably in coffins), and they partied hard all night, every night, making fools out of themselves.

Why Teener or anyone thought that I would ever hang out with them was beyond me.

"You've received some bad information," I told them, regaining my composure. "I have higher aspirations than making it onto *US Weekly's* worst-dressed list."

The Teener and her companions didn't care what I had to say. I don't even think they heard me. They were way too into their story to actually care if it was true or not. From the spaced-out look of glee on the Teener's face, I had a sinking feeling that the story got worse.

"Well," the Teener said, "we heard you were at Club Halo last night, dancing on a tabletop with *no underpants on.*"

Without meaning to, I let out a shriek.

"Listen, Teeny," I said coldly, "I went to bed at nine-thirty last night."

They all just laughed. They didn't believe me! I could feel my blood beginning to boil.

"Someone must have slipped some crack into your Bugles," I finally snapped. "Because I would never hang with the Stratfords. And anyone spreading rumors to the contrary is out of her mind." I stalked away and pulled the door to the next car open, making an escape.

It takes forever to ride the subway to the Halo City Department of Motor Vehicles. It's in a gloomy, out-of-the-way neighborhood full of warehouses and junkyards and God knows what. Every corner has some barking rottweiler throwing itself against a chain-link fence in an attempt to eat you alive.

Once you find your way inside the actual office, it's a lot shinier and more official seeming than the surrounding neighborhood—but it's no less depressing. It's like being inside an old Nintendo game with terrible graphics and that annoying, blippy music. You have to stand in line for an hour and then, when you make it through that line, they send you to another even longer line. So you're bounced around like Super Mario in the land of the bureaucratic nightmare.

The whole experience takes an entire afternoon, and that's assuming you actually get through it at all. Two out of the three times I'd tried it before, after making it all the way to the head of the second line, I'd been sent home for some idiotic infraction—like I forgot to bring a copy of my great-grandmother's immigration papers or I was wearing white go-go boots in winter. Stuff like that.

I think they design the system purposely to screw with you, because if it's too easy, if you had those spare hours back, you might use the time to try to overthrow the government or invent a tasty, nonfattening alternative to high-fructose corn syrup, thus wreaking total havoc on the U.S. economy.

Anyway, the point is that when you need to replace your driver's license you must bring a book, or at least a *Vanity Fair,* to the DMV. I hadn't brought either of those things. All I could do was wait.

The problem was, the more I waited, the more focused I became on the mystery at hand. Or rather, *mysteries.*

There was the missing purse, the anonymous phone call, the weird girl known as Sally Hansen, the disappearance of Berlin Silver, and—scariest of all—the dead shark girl. They had to be related to one another—except maybe Sally Hansen—but for the most part, I couldn't figure out how.

With nothing left to do and facing an endless wait, I whipped out my cell phone and called Daisy, who was busy at home, baking an angel food cake for her aunt's birthday. I filled her in on the events of last night—and this morning.

She thought the tattoo thing was weird, but she didn't think, at first, that I should worry about the phone call.

"Are you sure it wasn't just part of your nightmare?" she asked. "You know how sometimes you think you're awake, but you're actually still dreaming?"

"Daisy," I said firmly. "It was not a dream. Someone with my voice, claiming to be me, called me at four o'clock in the morning, insisting that I had her cell phone. *My* cell phone, I mean. What is going on?"

She paused, then had an idea. "Okay," she said, shouting over the noisy whir of an electric beater. "What if it was Rachel? Charlie told me that you ran into her last night and that she had some kind of bone to pick."

"Rachel?" I asked doubtfully. "Why would she have made a stupid call like that? I mean, why pretend to be me? Couldn't she have just asked if my refrigerator was running or something?"

"I don't know—why does Rachel do anything? She's crazy; you know that better than I do." There was the clatter of cookware and then the distinct crack of an eggshell.

Why did Daisy always have to be so sensible? As usual, she had come up with a much better explanation than I had. And unlike Charlie, she was almost managing to make me feel better. As we mulled over the idea that Rachel was responsible for the phone call, I realized that I'd never completely ruled out the possibility that she was the one who had stolen my purse, too.

"You know, maybe you're right," I said. "In which case, I'm just overreacting about that call. Well, I'm done. Rachel can bug me all she wants. I'm just going to ignore her and maybe she'll go away."

"Good idea," Daisy said.

But then I thought a little harder.

"Wait a minute. That still makes no sense. Even if Rachel did make the phone call, Genevieve still saw *Berlin* with my purse. And then there's the dead girl with the tattoo, and Berlin's ransacked room, and Sally Hansen, and . . ." I was about to start hyperventilating.

Daisy sighed. "I suppose you have a point. Something strange *is* going on. I wouldn't go so far as to suspect murder, but . . . I wish I was there with you now, Lulu. You're in a sketchy neighborhood. Be careful. I don't want you to turn up decapitated in the back of a Chevy Caprice."

"Thanks, Daisy. That's, like, such a comforting thought."

"Oh, I'm just joking," she said, with a nervous chuckle. Then added, "Sort of. So listen, I'm working tonight. Why don't you and Charlie come over to Little Edie's and we'll all sit down and figure things out?"

"Okay," I agreed.

Daisy and I continued talking for the greater part of an hour. My dad was going to kill me when he got the bill, but what else was I supposed to do? The line for a new driver's license was moving ever so slowly. While we talked, I fidgeted, hopped up and down in place, fiddled with my hair, and I'm sure drove all the other misbegotten DMV patrons crazy.

I heard a timer ding in the background. "Cake's done. I have to go," Daisy said.

"No! Don't leave me!" I whined.

"Lulu, don't worry, you're going to be fine," Daisy said. "I have confidence in you. And obviously if someone attacks you, you know that the most prudent thing to do is to turn your enemy's own strength against her. Like, okay, if she rushes you with a machete, or one of those big, round hammers with spikes all over it, or a battle-ax or something, what you do is grab her under the—"

There was a sizzle of static.

"Daisy? Wait—Daisy? I can't hear you!" I checked the phone's display. The line was dead.

Great. I was out of batteries. Now I would never know what to do if my enemy rushed me with a battle-ax.

Even though she'd been trying to comfort me, Daisy had just gotten me more worked up. With no further recourse for distraction, I was pulled into my own imagination.

I was thinking about dead girls and stolen driver's licenses and evil clones of all sorts. Teenage shark witches floating in the bay, green and decaying, blue hair full of seaweed, just itching to pull another victim down into their watery sisterhood.

If the shark girl in the police morgue wasn't Berlin, who could it be?

Maybe it was the phone call I'd gotten or the fact that I was standing in line to get a new ID, but I started wondering, what makes someone herself? If you get your driver's license stolen, or you put it through the laundry one too many times, or you never bother to get one in the first place, are you still you? If you have nothing to prove it to anyone, how can anyone be sure of who you are? Is it your clothes, or your hairdo, or your voice, or what?

Deep down I knew that it was your friends. My friends, I mean. I was sure that no matter what, Daisy, Charlie, my dad—and maybe even Genevieve—would always know me. I could go into the witness protection program, get radical plastic surgery, cut off all my hair, cover my body in tattoos, *whatever:* they would track me down and each of them would recognize me without a moment's hesitation. With their eyes closed, their hands tied behind their backs.

That thought was a comfort, but it made me sad, too, because Berlin didn't have that. In some ways I was the closest it got for her, and I was looking for her for purely selfish reasons. I wasn't a real friend—or even a fake friend. I just wanted my purse back! No one else was even curious about her disappearance; no one else seemed to have noticed that she was missing.

If what Charlie's friend Adam had told us was true, even her parents were blissfully ignorant—somewhere on the other side of the world while their daughter was most likely dead.

I knew then that as much as I did *not* want to be a girl detective, I had a responsibility to get to the bottom of things. Because no one else was going to do it, and even if Berlin was a bitch, no one, absolutely no one, deserves to die by herself. It was an issue of fairness and justice.

No, I told myself, *I am not a girl detective. But I care about truth, and, you know, justice and all that. I am not about to stand by and let bad stuff go down.*

That was it the key thing. Here I had been pondering these silly questions about what made me *me* when I knew the answer all along. I was Lulu Dark, and no one could take that away from me. I only wished that Berlin could have had the same luxury.

"Next!" a clerk behind the DMV counter called.

The small bald man behind me gave me a poke on the shoulder.

"Next!" the clerk called again.

I blinked. I had been lost in the mysteries of the universe for so long that miraculously, I hadn't even noticed I'd made it to the front of the line! Before I knew it, I was facing down the surly DMV clerk, answering her clueless questions, and finally sitting in front of the blue screen for my new picture.

I was prepared for the snapshot to be terrible, because although I consider myself to be dead sexy in real life, I'm one of the most unphotogenic people alive, which is sort of funny considering that I myself am a brilliant photographer.

It's just that when I'm on the other side of the lens, I get so nervous. It always takes longer than I'm expecting for the flash to go off, and when it finally happens, I'm caught in between two totally dopey expressions, which, together, never fail to add up to the "I just farted" face.

This time, though, things were different. Unbelievably, the picture was great. I looked like nothing other than my most perfect self. A sweet, killer scowl played on my lips and my dark, wavy hair framed my face in an unstudied lion's mane.

I was going to hold on to this driver's license until the end of time, long after it expired. Because in this very picture, I was starting to figure myself out.

And that was the meaning of hot.

I didn't know what last night's prank caller was playing at, but she was pretending to be me, and that was not okay.

Besides, what was the point? Was I supposed to say, *That's right, you're Lulu Dark, and I must have been mistaken about it for the last sixteen and a half years*?

Was the caller trying to scare me? Intimidate me?

It was mysterious, but I knew I would get to the bottom of it. For the first time in a week I had confidence pumping blood to brain.

Nothing lasts long, though, especially certainty. It's like water in the desert—gone before you know it. And before you realize what's happening, you're parched again, looking for a new oasis.

My rude awakening came while I was on the train heading back downtown. I was just standing there, turning my new license back and forth, admiring the picture, when I looked up and saw, for the second time in one day, *Sally Hansen!* She was standing on the platform, waiting for the train doors to open.

I quickly elbowed my way to a back corner and stood behind a heavyset businessman reading a copy of the *Halo City Times*. I crouched down and peered over the edge of his paper. Sally was getting on the train.

Seeing her once today had been jarring enough. Now I was downright frightened. This girl was totally following me. Luckily she didn't appear to be aware of my hiding spot. She had pulled out a magazine and was leaning against the door on the far side of the car.

It seemed possible that she was trying to look inconspicuous, although that would have been hard in the outfit she was wearing. She was all high-glam lunacy—with caked-on Cleopatra eyeliner, cartoon cleavage, and platinum hair teased into a white-blond nimbus. She was wearing pink hot pants and gold stiletto heels that laced all the way up her calves. Naturally, her French manicure was impeccably maintained.

I took out my notebook. *SALLY HANSEN— PINK HOT PANTS!!!* I scribbled, adding a third exclamation point to emphasize that this was my fourth run-in with the obsessive filer. You never knew when such information would come in handy.

I tried not to panic. Other than calling me a cow and shooting death rays at me with those heavily masacara'd eyes, she hadn't actually done anything to me. Not yet. And at least she wasn't carrying a machete or a battle-ax.

I was straining to see what magazine she was reading when my businessman camouflage abruptly closed his paper and shuffled off the train, leaving me an open target. I freaked and leapt behind a small elderly woman chewing a wad of gum.

"Excuse me," the old lady hollered, calling the attention of the entire car. Sally's head shot up and she looked me right in the eye.

The train was about to pull out of the station, so I made a furious break for the door, hoping that I could lose her. As I rushed through the turnstile, out of the station, I looked over my shoulder and saw that she had managed to make it out of the train too.

Sweat formed on my forehead. There was no doubt about it now. I was being followed by a manicure-crazed, hot-pants-wearing freak. A freak who *could* be a murderer!

SEVEN WITH SALLY ON MY TRAIL, I

scurried up the subway stairs.

What was I going to do? In my eagerness to escape, I'd paid no heed to what stop the train was at. Now, in the street, I realized that I was totally unfamiliar with this neighborhood.

Rushing along the sidewalk, pushing through crowds of people, I remembered something that freaked me out even more—something that I'd totally forgotten. Sally Hansen had talked to Berlin Silver on the night of the Many Handsomes show.

It was too strange to be coincidental. Sally Hansen, I instantly felt sure, had to be Berlin Silver's killer and the girl on the phone, too. Now she was coming after *me!*

I glanced over my shoulder without breaking stride. Sally Hansen wasn't ten feet behind me. How could she move so fast in those six-inch heels? Did she wear them on the treadmill at the gym?

My skin broke out in goose bumps at the thought of her shoes. If Sally cornered me, she'd be able to do some serious bodily harm with the spikes on her feet.

Death by high heel. It wouldn't be a pretty sight.

Sally was bearing down on me, and I needed to get away!

It had grown dark out and everything in the neighborhood seemed to be on my evil pursuer's side, from the garish, fun-house faces of the tourists on the street corners to the spiderwebs of hissing power lines that hovered low over my head. Everything in my path seemed to be whispering to me, telling me to give it up, saying that I'd be joining the shark girl in no time at all.

I made a hairpin turn onto a dark side street, hoping that Sally would just speed past. But she was right there, in hot pursuit, attempting to catch up. There was nothing else to do. I broke into a run.

The clatter of galloping heels sounded behind me. Sally wasn't giving up. I needed someplace to hide. And fast!

I turned sharply at the next corner—and a feeling of amazement washed over me. I recognized this place! Somehow, without knowing what I was doing, I'd made it to the heart of Marisol's neighborhood. Her apartment was no more than a block away.

True, she couldn't exactly be considered a friend, but she'd been nice enough to me the last time I'd shown up on her doorstep, and she surely would take pity on someone who was marked for death. All I had to do was outpace Sally Hansen.

It took every ounce of fortitude that I had, but I ran faster— then even faster. My muscles burned as my feet pounded the cement. When I finally stumbled into the doorway of Marisol's building, I'd managed to put quite a bit of distance between myself and the murderess. I could only pray that I'd have enough time to get buzzed in before meeting my demise at the tip of a designer stiletto.

Thank goodness for the casual goodwill of Marisol's hippie family. Like last time, the door clicked open with a blessed snap just seconds after I rang the buzzer. I slipped breathlessly through the entry and pressed myself against the wall. Through the small window in the front door I watched Sally Hansen race by with a confused look on her face. She hadn't noticed me enter the building.

With my heart about to give out, I took the stairs to Marisol's apartment two at a time, spiraling upward to safety.

Sunny, Marisol's mom, greeted me at the top of the stairwell with a questioning expression.

"Are you here to see Marisol again?" she asked.

"I am so glad to see you," I said breathlessly, not quite answering her question. "I have just had the worst day ever." I was trying to sound casual, but when I looked down, my hands were shaking.

Sunny didn't say anything—she just reached out and gave me a big hug.

Then and there I decided that hippies are the greatest people on earth. Sunny didn't seem to think it was weird that an almost stranger had shown up out of nowhere, looking for hugs. She just gave them. And believe me, it helped.

"It's going to be okay," Sunny said. Her voice was the warmest sound I'd heard in a while. "Come inside. We'll work it all out."

When I followed Sunny into the apartment, I couldn't help feeling embarrassed. I was usually known for being unflappable, and here I was, having a total freak-out in front of Marisol Bloom's mother.

As if by magic, Sunny already had the teakettle boiling, and she told me to sit. I slid onto the couch and she brought us each a mug—with a third for Marisol, who had emerged from her bedroom and perched next to me on the couch. She didn't say anything, but she was obviously brimming with curiosity.

Half-assedly, I attempted to clean myself up, but it was pretty pointless. I was soaked with sweat, and my hair—let's not even get into my hair.

"Tell us everything," Sunny said, settling down into a big wicker chair, tucking the heels of her bare feet under herself.

I recounted the entire frightening story while they listened in horrified astonishment. When I was done, I felt exhausted all over again, limbs aching and brain throbbing.

"Wow," Marisol said. "That's so messed up. I wish I'd seen who took your purse, but I know for sure it wasn't Rachel."

Sunny was biting her nails. Slowly she spoke. "I'll help as much as I can," she said, in her awesome earth mother drawl. "But the best I can do is a little psychic counsel."

"You're psychic?" I asked.

"Of course I am," she replied. "Couldn't you tell?"

I had never believed in that stuff before, but that night, in Marisol's apartment, I was ready to take what I could get. And with the incense, the tall yellow candles, and the hippie artwork everywhere, a little mystical mumbo jumbo didn't seem that far-fetched.

"Let me get my tarot cards," Sunny said, and hopped up with a new purpose. She came back from the bedroom, carrying a red silk bag, which she dumped out onto the low circular coffee table. "Shuffle," she said.

I looked over at Marisol. She had a funny red-faced smile, like she couldn't decide whether to be embarrassed or proud.

Unsure of what to expect, I gathered the cards in my hands and slowly shuffled. I thought about trying some of my fancy card shark moves but figured it might mess with the voodoo. I kept it simple.

"Now, while you're shuffling, think about the events of the past week or two," Sunny instructed. "Silently ask your subconscious for clarity and understanding."

I closed my eyes and thought hard about everything. I focused on Berlin and Sally Hansen, on Alfy Romero and the dead body, the shark tattoo and the phone call and the chase I'd just been through. For some reason, I thought about Charlie, too, and about my purse. I was totally zoning out when from nowhere, the image of that shiny, rhinestone-studded necklace popped into my mind and stuck. HATTIE. Up until now, I'd forgotten all about it.

I couldn't say how long I shuffled those cards. It could have been ten seconds or it could have been ten minutes. I had drifted into a trancelike state when the deck seemed to just spring from my hands onto the table.

"Good, good," Sunny said when I opened my eyes. "I'm getting some excellent vibes from you."

She picked up the cards and began dealing them faceup in the shape of a cross. As she did it, her eyes widened.

"Don't freak out," she murmured. "This is pretty intense."

She didn't have to tell me that. I was looking at the cards as she dealt them, and let me tell you, it didn't seem like anything good. I knew that tarot cards could be freaky, but from the top of the pile, through Sunny's hands, cards with gory pictures and names like Death and The Devil were appearing in my reading. I had to remind myself to breathe.

Marisol put her hand on my shoulder. "Don't worry, Lulu. It's not as bad as it looks."

"You are the Princess of Swords," Sunny said. She pointed at a card in the middle of the layout, which pictured a girl with a huge saber in her hand, ready for battle. "It's in the identity position of your spread, but I knew you were her the minute I saw you. Before you ever said a word. It's an amazing card, Lulu. It doesn't really tell us anything that we didn't already know, just that you're powerful. It's a card of wisdom and determination. You have a lot of knowledge, sometimes more than you can handle. And more than others can handle too. You have a tendency to rub people the wrong way."

Marisol was covering her mouth, trying to hide some kind of amusement.

"So I'm a smart, overbearing bitch?" I asked, feeling insulted. What was so great about that?

"Your spirit makes people uncomfortable," Sunny corrected me. "But it's an incredible weapon. You can always rely on it, and you have to remember that. As long as you know your own strength, you can be unstoppable."

Now Marisol was laughing out loud.

"What?" I asked her testily.

"You and Rachel have the same card," she said. "Rachel's the Princess of Swords too."

"Why is that funny?" Sunny asked.

"Rachel and Lulu hate each other."

"Well, that doesn't surprise me," Sunny said with a smile. "Two princesses in the same room? It can get messy."

"O-*kay*," I said, trying not to be crabby. With the events of the day, not to mention the whole last week, Rachel was the last person on my mind. "What about the *mystery?*"

Sunny studied the cards some more, squinting hard in thought. She took a deep breath. "Now the bad news. You're in danger, Lulu. That's clear. Death, the Tower, the Devil, the Moon. The trouble you're facing isn't in your imagination. But just so you know, this Death card, it doesn't really mean anyone is going to die. It's about the end of one thing and the start of another. Imagine a door closing and another opening. Rebirth. It's actually a good card a lot of the time."

I couldn't tell if she was for real or if she was just trying to make me feel better. These New Age people think they can turn anything into something positive. Like they stub their toe and consider it to be spiritually cleansing or something.

"Now the Devil card and the Moon; the Tower. Those are another story. None of them are terrible by themselves, and they're not necessarily terrible now either, but they show me that trouble and secrets are surrounding you. You're caught up in something that you can't control or understand. The Tower foresees disaster and destruction. A tumble. Things are going to get worse before they get better."

I groaned. I couldn't really imagine how things could get much worse.

"Do you want to see what you're up against?"

"Maybe?" I said weakly.

"It's a big one. The Magician. He's the master of deception, Lulu. He's an expert at every trick there is. You'll need to marshal all your courage and intellect—all your fierceness—to defeat him."

"Are you kidding me?" I looked at Sunny incredulously. Her tarot reading was foretelling nothing but bad news.

"I'm not going to lie," she told me. "It's a tall order. Everything I see shows that you have a hard road ahead. But the cards are also telling me that it's something you have to face. You'll come out of it bigger than before. Can I give you some advice, Lulu?"

I nodded, still unconvinced. I briefly considered picking up and moving someplace very remote, like Greenland or Boston. But, I reminded myself, if I did that, I would never find out the truth. And that was the most important thing of all.

Sunny pointed, with her thumb and pinky, to two adjacent cards: Judgment and the Ten of Cups. "These are the cards that you need to keep in mind if you're going to get through this. I know you can do it, and the cards know it too. First, the Ten of Cups. It's the card of friendship. You're strong on your own, Lulu, but you're far stronger when you're surrounded by friends.

You won't be able to accomplish anything without the help of others."

That made sense, but it wasn't really anything new. I'd always relied on Charlie and Daisy for everything, and that wasn't about to change.

"Now Judgment. See the picture on this card?"

It showed eight naked people rising up out of their graves toward an angel in the sky. I made a face. The naked people were kind of ugly—in that medieval way, with a bit of pudge—and really, who wants to see that?

"This card is telling you not to be deceived by outward appearances," Sunny explained. "Your own or anyone else's. It's about inner sight. Remember yourself always—who you are and why you are. More importantly, though, remember who others are. People are more complicated than they look on the outside and it's easy to forget that. Use your intellect. See past falseness. You have all the tools you need, but you can't just let them lie there. Pick up the sword, Lulu. It's lying right next to you."

I didn't know what to say. It was hard to interpret what Sunny had actually told me. Maybe it meant everything—maybe nothing. Like I say, this New Age business is mostly junk, right?

"I—I'll try," I finally said, noncommittal.

"You can do it," Sunny said. "You're the Princess of Swords."

I had to admit that even if I didn't know about the rest of the reading, that sword part was kind of cool. Being a princess seemed fun, especially a princess with a big fancy weapon. Maybe I could solve this mystery after all.

"Thanks," I said, and moved to stand.

"Hold on," Sunny told me. "One more thing. How's your love life, Lulu?"

I snorted. "Deceased," I said.

"I wouldn't be too sure about that." Sandy pointed at a card. "This is the Knight of Cups—right next to the Ten of Cups, reversed. The Knight of Cups is someone, a boy, usually, who is generous and kind and more than a little naive. Really, he's someone who can balance you. The fact that it's in this position, upside down, tells me that there's potential for great love but that there is some obstacle in the way. I think the obstacle is probably you—you're not seeing things properly. You're closing yourself off."

I thought about it. Was she talking about Alfy Romero? That didn't make sense. I was totally open to going out with Alfy. *He* was the one who wasn't seeing things properly. I was about to tell Sunny that maybe the obstacle was the fact that Alfy was too dim to even remember my face, but despite the fact that I'd spilled my guts to these two, there were some things that I still wanted to keep private.

"Hmm," I mumbled, trying my best to be vague.

It was getting late. The incense in the corner had burned itself out, and the candles were down to the nubs. I had to get going, but I was a little afraid of trying to go home all by myself.

More than a little, actually. More like terrified.

"Thanks for helping me out, Sunny," I said. "It means a lot."

I turned to Marisol. "Thanks," I told her. I owed her big time, but I didn't want to lay it on too thick.

"Whatever, Lulu," she said. "Anything I can do. Just promise you'll pay me back someday. Sooner rather than later." She broke into a big grin and gave me a hug. I didn't want to leave; I would have been perfectly content to spend the rest of my life in the Blooms' living room, drinking tea and talking about global warming or whatever hippies talk about when they're not being psychic. But I knew that it was time to get home. I was supposed to meet Daisy and Charlie at Little Edie's later that night. I knew that between the three of us, we would be able to figure out a logical explanation for everything that had happened. In the meantime, my hair needed some serious attention.

"Do you want us to call you a cab?" Sunny offered. "After what happened today, you shouldn't be wandering around Halo City all by yourself."

"That's okay," I told her. An idea popped into my head and cheered me up. "I'm going to call a friend of mine to come get me."

"That's good," Sunny said. "Already following the cards' advice."

I wasn't sure what she was on about, but whatever. I slipped into the kitchen and punched up Charlie on my cell.

"What's up, Lulu?" he buzzed.

"Charlie, I need some help."

"Hold on, I'm eating at Le Pince Nez with my grandparents."

There was some shuffling while he excused himself from the table. Charlie's grandparents are kind of snooty, but he has to be nice to them because, you know, they're related.

"Okay, what's wrong?"

I gave him the story in a nutshell, trying not to be too hysterical about it. There was a long pause on the other end. He didn't know what to say.

"Look," he finally decided, "I'm going to call my dad and get you a car for the night. You can't be walking around by yourself with all this going on. I'd come get you myself, but you know. Grandparents just don't understand."

"Charlie," I said, "you're awesome."

"Quit it," he told me firmly. "The car will be at Marisol's in ten minutes."

That's what I love about him. He'll be generous as hell, but you have to look in the other direction or it makes him uncomfortable.

I couldn't help grinning as I hung up the phone.

Marisol and I went out front and waited together. Any animosity she'd had toward me seemed to have been replaced by sympathy. As for me, there was no way I would ever be mean to her, or by extension Rachel, again. After all she'd done for me, I owed her that much.

"Hey," I said remembering the scene at Medardo. "Can you tell Rachel that I wasn't talking about her behind her back? I don't know where she got that idea, but she was really mad about it last night. I know she doesn't have much of a reason to believe me, but I swear I haven't been. And I'm sorry I suspected her of taking my purse."

"You mean you *haven't* been telling everyone that she has a third nipple?" Marisol was dubious.

"No way!" I said. "Where on earth did she get that idea?"

"Millie Stratford told us. She said that she was at some party with you the other night and that you couldn't stop talking about Rachel's third nipple. She said you told her it looked like a pink Mike and Ike, right in the middle of her chest."

Normally it would have been hard to keep a straight face at the thought of that, but I was too annoyed by the first part of the news to be amused.

"*Millie Stratford?* I don't think I've spoken three words to her in my entire life," I defended myself. "And I haven't been to a party in weeks. I've been too busy obsessing over my purse."

"That's strange," Marisol said thoughtfully.

But it was more than strange. It was the second time that someone had accused me of hanging out with the Stratfords in the space of one day. I didn't know what to make of it, but combined with everything else that was going on, it was beyond bizarre.

From my back pocket I retrieved my notebook. *FRIENDS WITH THE STRATFORD TWINS?!* I jotted furiously. *AS IF!*

Marisol gave me a curious look. "Taking up journaling?" she said, half teasing.

I scoffed. "I just have a bad memory, okay? It's not like it's a diary or something. Jeez."

There was a rumble and a huge, sparkling white limousine came rolling smoothly around the corner. It stopped right in front of me, and a chauffeur in a tuxedo stepped out and walked around to the passenger side.

"Ms. Dark?" the man boomed in a smooth baritone.

I was dumbfounded. A white limo? It must be Charlie's idea of a joke. What was this, *Pretty Woman?* I had to give it to him—he knew how to cheer a girl up.

Marisol gave me a wide-eyed smirk. "Friends in high places, huh?"

I tossed my hair like a movie star, gave Marisol my best Hollywood air kiss, and stepped up to the car with mock haughtiness.

The driver opened the door for me. A moment later we were off.

As the car drifted along the glittery Halo City avenues, I imagined myself as the Princess of Swords, carried in my royal chariot. I lay back, put my feet up on the seat, and lounged on the white leather upholstery. I picked up the car phone and found, to my amazement, that there was a dial tone. Impulsively I called my mother in California. Maybe she would have some advice about all this.

"Mom!" I said excitedly when she answered. "I'm in a white stretch limo!"

"That's a weird coincidence," she said breezily. "So am I. One of those big ones that sort of look like pickup trucks."

I was put off. Leave it to Isabelle Dark to steal my thunder.

"Why are *you* in a white stretch SUV?" I asked.

"Penelope Cruz sent it for me. We're having a get-together in Malibu. I'm playing her secretary in this movie—some fake-o artsy neo-noir. You know the drill."

"Do you die?" I asked, already knowing the answer.

"She stabs me with my own letter opener," she admitted, slightly dejected. Then she brightened. "It's the climax of the first act, though. My death scene is going to be brilliant. Lots of eye rolling and wheezing. Like this." There was a long, strangled noise from California. I held the phone a few inches away from my ear while my mom *ack-argh-hack-hack-argh*ed. The icing on the histrionics was a high-pitched, thirty-second scream that slowly faded to a gurgle.

"How do you like it?" she finally asked, finished.

"Great, Mom. You'll be great."

"Too bad you couldn't see the eye rolls. They're the best part. It's not like I'm going to win an Oscar, but it's all about your personal best, you know? That's what they always tell you at those change-your-life seminars. Don't try to compete with others; compete with yourself. It's always middle-aged B actresses at those things, by the way. I wonder why. So how are you?"

"Fine," I said. "I just wanted to tell you that I was in a white stretch limo."

"Well, enjoy," she said. "But don't stick your head out the sunroof. I knew this poor girl who got decapitated that way. She could have been famous if only she hadn't stuck her head out the sunroof."

"C'mon, Mom, it's not like I'm at some tacky bachelorette party," I said. "Have a little faith."

"I have all the faith in the world when it comes to you. You know your mom, though, always fussing over nothing."

"Listen, Mom, could you give me some advice about something?"

"Of course, darling. What do you need to know? I hope it's not to do with getting a stain out of your dress because I'm really not good with that Hints from Heloise stuff."

"Well—" I began, but I didn't get to finish my sentence.

"Sorry, babe," Isabelle said. "I'm going to have to cut this short. I'm here at Penelope's."

"Okay, Mom," I said, resigned. "Talk to you soon."

"You too, honey." And *click*.

It was a typical conversation with Isabelle. Her head is always in the clouds, if not on the moon. It's not like she doesn't love me; it's just that she never seems to pay any attention to what I have to say. If I'd bothered to tell her that I was being pursued by an evil murderesses in pink hot pants, she probably would have laughed and told me about some movie where she had to die while wearing hot pants herself. *Oh, well,* I thought—at least there was Dad. That was more than a lot of people could say. For instance, Daisy. *Both* of her parents are crazy.

I took out my notebook and wrote, *CHILDBIRTH AND INSANITY. IS THERE A MEDICAL CONNECTION?*

Signs pointed to yes.

The limo dropped me off in front of my house, and the chauffeur idled across the street. He'd be there as long as I needed him. This was the life.

Back in the loft, there was a note from my dad on the kitchen counter. Somehow the fact that he and Theo were going to be out of town for a week at some big art opening had slipped my mind.

Lulu! the note read. *Have fun by yourself. No wild parties OR ELSE.*

Or parties of any kind, for that matter. The credit card's on the coffee table and there's plenty of food in the fridge. If you need anything, just call my celly. Be good, and if not, be careful. Love, Dad.

Crap. This was not what I needed when I was being pursued by a killer lunatic! Normally I would have been thrilled to have the apartment to myself, but under these circumstances? No way.

I was still studying the note when I felt a hand on my shoulder. "Aaaaaaaa!" I let out a bloodcurdling scream.

EIGHT I WHIRLED AROUND, READY TO

fight to the death.

Standing behind me was none other than Genevieve—with a very sour look on her face. Yeah, I know, you thought it was going to be Berlin's murderer. Well, needless to say, I'm happy it wasn't, but trust me, being snuck up on by Charlie's fink of a sister is almost as bad.

"Hello, Lulu," she said, glowering. "I think we need to have a little chat."

She was standing with her arms crossed, eyeing me up and down while I backed slowly toward the kitchen counter. I wasn't sure what was going on, but I knew it couldn't be anything good.

"What do you want?" I snapped. "And how did you get in here?" I was feeling a little paranoid, I guess.

Genevieve rolled her eyes. "Lulu, your dad let me in before he left. We need to talk."

"Talk about what?" I said with suspicion.

Genevieve smiled condescendingly. "Just a little girl talk, Lulu.

Woman-to-woman. Now, can you please chill out? You're being a real freak."

She was right; I was just on edge. "Okay, Genevi*evil*. Talk. But get to the point. I need to meet your brother in a few minutes."

"Fine," she said, sniffing. She put a hand on her hip and cocked her head. "I know that you and I don't always get along. But I respect you, sort of. And I'm concerned for my brother. You're being a real bitch to him, Lulu, and that's not okay. If you do anything to hurt him, then you and I are *really* going to have problems. Are we clear on that?"

I looked at her incredulously. "You're going to have to explain, Gen, because I have no idea what you're talking about."

"Listen, you obviously know that Charlie is completely in love with you. Everyone does." Genevieve looked at me meaningfully.

I blinked. *Everyone knew that Charlie was in love with me?* That was ridiculous! Just last night he made it perfectly clear that he only wanted to be friends.

I squinted at Genevieve. Someone in this room was smoking crack, and it definitely wasn't me.

"Anyway," Gen went on, "if you think you're too good for Charlie, you're obviously deluded. All I'm saying is that you'd better stop jerking him around like this. Seriously, you do not want to be on my bad side any more than you already are."

Jerking him around? This had to be some kind of joke.

I was so stressed out already—Charlie's alleged infatuation was the last thing I wanted to think about. My palms grew clammy and my stomach churned. This was worse than the time my dad decided

to sit me down and talk to me about my "cycles." I had to end this conversation. Quickly.

"Genevieve, I don't know where you're getting your information from, but Charlie is not in love with me. He told me only last night that we were just friends."

She raised her eyebrows at me like I was a moron. "Yeah, he told me all about last night, Lulu. You're sending him all kinds of mixed signals. Of course he wanted to save face."

I let out a groan and dragged myself over to the couch. I slumped down in it with my face in my hands. I had to collect my thoughts, and Genevieve was only making my brain more cluttered and confused.

"Gen, this is too much. I'm not trying to screw with Charlie's mind. In fact, maybe it's the other way around. I mean, when he dresses up and takes me out to Medardo only to tell me it's not a date, what am I supposed to think?"

Gen had followed me onto the couch. She sat next to me.

"Lulu." She sighed. "For such a know-it-all, your feminine intuition is seriously deficient."

"Feminine intuition is so sexist." I sniffed.

"Well, whatever. How do you feel about my brother?"

I threw my hands up in the air. "I don't know! I think Charlie's cute. I think he's great. I think he's the best friend I could ever ask for."

Genevieve twirled a tendril of her blond hair around her pinky finger. She looked at me appraisingly. "Fair enough," she finally said. "But you really need to talk about this with him or things are just

going to get worse. And if you hurt him . . ." She let her thought trail off, raising her eyebrows again.

I got the point.

"Fine," I moaned. "I'll talk to him."

Right about the time that hell freezes over, I added to myself.

Genevieve gave me a tentative smile and a pat on the knee. "Good. That's all I wanted to hear. In the meantime, as a gesture of goodwill, I'm going to give you a piece of information that you might find helpful: I was at Rhonda B's boutique yesterday, and one of the clerks mentioned that Berlin Silver had been in there recently. You might want to check it out."

"Berlin Silver?" I gasped. "Like, how recently?"

"Sometime in the last week," Genevieve reported. "Now, don't say I never did anything nice for you." She stood up, gave me a quick peck on the cheek, and was out the door without saying goodbye.

I closed my eyes and took a couple of deep, cleansing breaths. I was being tugged in so many directions—the thing with Sally Hansen, the stuff with Charlie, the situation with Berlin. I checked my watch. Rhonda B's was closed. I would have to head over tomorrow and see what they knew.

There was no way, though, that I was going to sleep in this apartment alone tonight. Daisy would just have to let me sleep over at her place whether Svenska liked it or not. I spruced myself up, packed an overnight bag as fast as I could, and hurried out the door.

In the limo I had a thought. I picked up the car phone and dialed Detective Wanda Knight.

"Detective, it's Lulu Dark," I said when she answered. "I need police protection."

I could hear the detective stifling a laugh on the other end. "What is it now, Lulu?" she asked.

After I told her about the incident with Sally Hansen, she sighed. "Lulu, I think you're overreacting. This young woman didn't even *say* anything to you."

"She didn't need to *say* anything!" I yelped. "She was trying to *kill* me."

"Well," Detective Knight said carefully, "I suppose you should be careful. You can call me if anything else happens. But unless this person threatens you directly, there's nothing I can do."

"You can't just give me one teensy police escort?" I whined.

Detective Knight laughed out loud this time. She wasn't trying to be mean, but I still didn't appreciate it.

"Maybe this will make you feel better," she said when she was done chortling. "Berlin Silver is alive and well. I paid a little visit to the Primrose Hotel for Young Ladies today. Melanie Raymond practically talked my ear off."

"What did she say about Berlin?" I cut to the chase.

"That Berlin called the hotel yesterday and told her she was moving out. A guy came and picked up all her stuff and everything. So the shark girl from the river isn't Berlin Silver—just as I told you. You can rest easy, Lulu. Your friend is fine."

I shook my head. This didn't add up. "Was Mel sure it was *really* Berlin?" I asked.

"She was positive. And you know, a woman like that, she doesn't miss a beat."

Sure, I thought. The woman who ran the Primrose Hotel missed just about every beat.

If Detective Knight or Mel hadn't seen Berlin in the flesh, I wasn't buying this story.

"Lulu," Detective Knight said, "I know you're on edge, but who knows why you keep seeing the same girl? Maybe she lives down the street from you. Maybe she wants to ask you where you got your glasses. Where did you get your glasses, by the way? They're very original."

"Halo Park Eyewear," I said. I could tell that she was just trying to cheer me up by complimenting me, and it wasn't going to work. "Well, thanks," I added.

"Buck up," she told me. "Berlin's fine. . . . You've got nothing to be concerned about."

I hung up with a sigh. A lot of help she was. Detective Knight seemed like a smart lady, but I still thought she was missing something. I just had to figure out what it was.

At Little Edie's, I felt slightly better. Seeing Daisy in full waitress mode is so amusing that it gave me a breather from all the day's puzzles.

That night she was jetting around the café with sparkling aplomb, balancing like five plates on each arm. I sat in my usual chair, waiting for Charlie to show. I was taking small sips from my coffee, trying to make it last because there was no way Daisy was getting around to giving me a refill.

The place was packed, and Katinka, the night manager, was playing hooky as usual. Her dad owns Little Edie's, making it her prerogative to never show up. As a result Daisy always ends up running the place herself, which is a little like putting the bull in charge of the china shop.

She was looking sporty that particular night, or at least Sporty Spice, in striped jogging shorts, a white T-shirt, flip-flops, and red terry-cloth wristbands. She glided around the place like some out-of-whack figure skater, keeping everyone waiting and mixing up all the orders. When Daisy is your waitress, you're lucky to get your food at all, but it's okay because of the adorable way she laughs and spins and tosses her ponytail.

You would think that Daisy being the manager would be a sure-fire recipe for disaster, but in the end it never failed to be fine. The cash register balanced itself; the dishes got done. Things fall into place for Daisy—they just do. She should take up gambling, I often think. Daisy would be the queen of the roulette wheel.

I'd been contenting myself for the past hour just people watching and trying to ignore the fact Charlie hadn't arrived. He was supposed to show up soon and—given my conversation with Genevieve—the last thing I wanted was for there to be awkwardness.

At the heart of it, though, I was anxious for him to walk through the door. I hoped that once I saw him, all this confusion between us would just melt away. I had no idea where things were going between us, but I was pretty sure I could count on him not to get all weird at a time when I needed him.

I focused my attention back onto the scene at Little Edie's. All the regulars were there, and they were a constant source of fascination. Daisy and I had given them all their own nicknames.

In the corner Doughnut and his red-faced girlfriend, Raspberry, were crammed together on the divan, deep in an ostentatious lip lock since my arrival. Right next to me, on a velvet ottoman, was the guy we called Aladdin. He always wore the same thing—a red sequined vest over a bare, flabby, plucked torso, accessorized with a golden fez the size of a Dixie cup. Aladdin was obsessed with word finds, the kind old ladies buy in books at the supermarket. He would sit at Little Edie's for hours, barely looking up, just flying through stacks of them.

I glanced at my watch again. Why was Charlie Reed always, *always* late?

I was getting totally bored. I needed a distraction.

Daisy, having a mild case of ESP, could tell I was getting antsy, so she put me to work for her. "Lulu!" she shouted from across the room. "How about finding these people seats?"

She pointed toward a bored cluster of biker ladies by the door.

Daisy was shimmying and bouncing to the song on the jukebox while she absentmindedly tossed the food in her arms onto random tables. I sighed and stood up to help.

I told Doughnut and Raspberry to get a room and moved Aladdin onto a makeshift seat to make room for the bikers. As I was handing them menus, Charlie breezed in, with Genevieve in tow. She was carrying her annoying Boston terrier, Viking, in a wicker picnic basket. I gave Genevieve a quick smile, which was returned with an icy, furious glare.

I shook my head. Sometimes I swear that girl is bipolar. Hadn't she been sort of *friendly* with me just an hour earlier?

I glanced at Charlie and gave him a tentative grin as well. Rather than reciprocating, he barely met my gaze.

"Lulu, my lady," he said, with a hint of sarcasm. "I've been hearing about your adventures."

"Ugh." I sighed. "It's been terrible."

"It didn't sound so terrible to me," he retorted.

I was about to correct Charlie when Viking freed himself from his carrier and began chewing on my ankle.

"Genevieve," I said, half jokingly, "all Vikings must control themselves or be sent to the pound."

"Oh, Lulu, you're such a little jokester." She scooped the dog into her arms and glared at me—again.

"Don't blame me," I told her, returning the mean look this time. "It's management policy."

I wanted to ask Charlie why, precisely, he thought that being chased by a killer sounded anything less than horrifying, but he had already moved on. He hated listening to me bicker with his sister, and from the looks of things, he was hungry. He stood and wandered the café, busing plates and eating the leftovers as he did it.

"Fried chicken?" he offered, sidling back over to us and hoisting a half-eaten drumstick in Genevieve's face.

She shuddered. "No, thank you."

Finally Daisy appeared from the kitchen. She threw her arms around me, Charlie, and Genevieve all at once, gathering us into a cramped embrace. My nose ground right into Genevieve's cheekbone.

"Friends!" Daisy proclaimed with a theatrical sigh. "Now the night is perfect."

She sent Lionel the cook home early and announced to the customers that the kitchen was closed. There was some grumbling throughout the place, but no one moved to leave. Daisy plopped the coffeepot down on the table. She perched herself on the windowsill while Charlie pulled up some chairs.

"Thank goodness that's over," Daisy said, stretching her arms to the ceiling. "All night it's all, 'Bring me food; bring me water; bring us the check.' Don't these people have mothers?"

Genevieve, who had ensconced herself regally in a throne-like armchair, snorted and set her dog loose again, much to the delight of the rest of the patrons. They didn't seem to realize what an obnoxious little rodent Viking was. When I looked over, the biker chicks had all turned to mush, cooing embarrassingly and feeding him french fries. "So Lulu," Charlie said. His voice was even. "Tell us about your wild Friday night."

Genevieve gave me a wan smile, drumming her vampy red talons on the table in expectation. Daisy leaned forward eagerly, looking back and forth at the three of us. "I didn't hear about this part," she said, already famished for fresh gossip.

"My wild Friday night?" I asked, confused. "You were with me Friday night. You know as well as I do that it was the opposite of wild."

"Yeah. Sure," Charlie grumbled.

Genevieve couldn't contain herself. "Lulu, *everyone* is talking about you—saying you're trying to make a name for yourself as bimbo of the month." She sneered, and I sneered back. It was one thing for Genevieve to be bitchy to me—that was the normal course of events. But when I looked at Charlie, he seemed genuinely pissed as well. He hadn't cracked a smile yet—just sat there stony-faced, staring with what I interpreted as low-level malice.

I tried to offer an olive branch, even though I had no idea what was eating him—or what Genevieve was talking about.

"Thanks for the limo, Charlie," I said. "It's been a lifesaver."

"Yeah, well," Charlie said. "A stretch limo should come in handy for your social exploits. I bet the Stratford twins love it."

That was it. I slammed my coffee cup down on the table. "Okay. For the last time today I am not, I repeat, *not* friends with the Stratford girls! I haven't even laid eyes on them since Genevieve's Halloween party. Yet everyone in Halo City seems to think that we're tight. So someone, please tell me what is going on here!?"

Daisy was leaning so far into the table that it looked like she was going to fall face-first into the coffeepot. Her eyes were big and incredulous. She was eating this up.

"Tell!" she squealed at Genevieve. "Tell!"

She Who Should Not Be Named shifted prissily in her seat, gearing up for a doozy. "Well," she said. "I saw Wendy Levine about *an hour ago*." Genevieve paused, narrowing her eyes at me before continuing. "Wendy told me that Lulu was spotted at Club Halo last night with Mr. Many Handsomes himself—and that she was making out with Alfy Romero in every manner imaginable. Borderline X-rated, you might say."

"Congratulations, Lulu," Charlie snapped as he stood. "I can see tomorrow's headline already: ART SCION AND ROCK STUD—A MATCH MADE IN MAKE-OUT HEAVEN."

With that he stomped out of the café and Genevieve stormed along behind him, leaving me with my mouth hanging open, still staring at their vacant seats.

NINE

NOTHING GETS ME OUT OF BED before noon on a Sunday morning. I get so little sleep during the week that I make up for it in spades when the weekend comes. This Sunday, however, was different. How could I sleep after Charlie's little scene the night before? Not only was I the only person aware of Berlin Silver's death, but someone was putting some serious effort into ruining my rep. Something had to be done.

It was ten o'clock. I'd been up for close to an hour, and I'd already gone through an elaborate beauty routine. Normally I'm pretty low-maintenance (with the exception of my all-important eye makeup and lip gloss), but on the off chance that I ran into Sally Hansen again and met my untimely demise, I was going to look good doing it. So I'd flat-ironed my hair and put on my Sunday best—my tinted sunglasses, cowboy boots, a summery blouse, a pair of white corduroy shorts, and around my waist, fashioned into a belt, a vintage Pucci scarf from the sixties. The scarf had been my mom's. She'd actually worn it in her first movie, the one where she got to be the ingenue, and it was kind of a lucky charm for me.

It was not only a stylish outfit, but a functional one. The shorts gave me the freedom of movement to run if I needed to. The sunglasses would augment my already-killer deadpan. And the steel-toed cowboy boots were my self-defense. As an afterthought, I used a pink ribbon to wrap my dark hair into a high ponytail for that intimidating Amazon look.

Mornings may not be my best time, but that's a gross understatement when it comes to Daisy. In fact, she's usually downright catatonic when she wakes up. Nonetheless, we had a lot of work to do, so I tried valiantly to rouse her. She was coming with me, even if it was in her pajamas.

Daisy loves to sleep so much that she does it under a lavish canopy, bedecked with plush, high-thread-count bedclothes. She wears a beauty mask and earplugs.

In slumber Daisy has the benign placidness of Sleeping Beauty, and she's just as unwakable. Unfortunately, I'm about as far as you can get from Prince Charming.

I tried to be kind at first, turning on perky classical music and pulling the shades open to let the sun in. Gingerly I removed Daisy's mask and then, disgusted, coaxed the earplugs from her ears. Ick.

"Daisy," I whispered in her ear. "Up and at 'em."

In her sleep she groaned and muttered something unintelligible.

"Time to pop up like a piece of toast and bounce out of bed like a rubber ball," I said louder, cringing inwardly at my own mixed metaphor.

"No!" Daisy shouted. I jumped back, but I wasn't quick enough.

Daisy's fist shot from its peaceful position under the covers and clocked me upside the head. Ouch!

Daisy snored. She was still asleep.

Whatever, I thought, rubbing my jaw. It was only a glancing blow, and maybe I'd look tough with a bruise.

I needed to try another tactic. Glancing around the room, I found a roll of gold wrapping paper and stood as far as I could from my sleeping friend. With the wrapping paper, I jabbed her sharply in the gut. Well, she *had* punched me. "Up, up, up, up, up!" I shouted.

In a trance Daisy sprang out of her bed. She wears this high-collared, flannel, old-woman nightgown. Her hair was pointing in every direction from her head, Gorgon-like. "Leemlong!" she shrieked. I interpreted this to mean "leave me alone."

Continuing to sputter in her half-dream state, Daisy came at me like a cyclone, all fists and flying spittle. I don't know how she knew where I was even standing: her eyes were still closed. Maybe she was guided by a dream. She chased me around the room, yelping wildly and trying to lay another punch anywhere she could connect while I staved her off with the wrapping paper tube. Finally, when she'd backed me into a corner, I hopped up on top of her desk, where she couldn't get me. "Mmmm nagggh," she spat, and collapsed on the floor in a heap. She began snoring again, loudly.

"Daisy!" I screamed at the top of my lungs.

Magically her eyes popped open. She rolled onto her back and looked up at me. Her scowl broadened into a beatific smile. "Lulu," she said sleepily. "What are you doing up there? We have work to do."

I was still afraid of the possibility of running into Sally Hansen, but with karate-chopping Daisy at my side I felt safe enough to get back on Berlin's trail.

On Genevieve's tip we took the limo to Third and Main, where Rhonda B's boutique is. Daisy had guzzled about a gallon of coffee and was now wired beyond belief. In her zeal she'd decided to dress like a spy for the day's high jinks. She wore a gray fedora, mirrored cat-eye sunglasses, and a formfitting trench coat that was shorter than I'm sure Svenska would have preferred.

Oh, how Daisy loves costumes.

As the limo rolled down State Street, I peered out the tinted windows, searching for any sign of the manicured menace.

"I don't see why you're so worried," Daisy said. "It's daytime—what can that girl do to you?"

"Kill me, of course," I said. "Murder can happen anytime, anyplace."

Daisy thought seriously about my aphorism. "I guess so," she said unsurely.

I decided to change the subject. "I still can't believe what happened with Charlie and Genevieve last night. I mean, what is with people wrecking my friendships by making up total lies about my personal life?"

"I'm not sure." Daisy shrugged. "Do you have a long-lost cousin who might be in town partying with the Stratfords? Because I once saw this episode of *The Patty Duke Show* where . . ." She trailed off, lost in the pleasant glow of a childhood spent in front of the television.

I shook my head. "Not possible. I am the sole progeny of the Dark clan. It's a lonely existence, but it rules around birthday time." I paused. "The thing is, there's so much happening at once. I think it's all related. But I can't figure out how. It's like, I can't see the big picture."

"Well, then, let's consider the things we already know," Daisy said. "Maybe everything will just fall into place. When I was taking the SATs and I couldn't figure out an answer, I'd just stare at the question for thirty seconds and then guess. I got a perfect score, so there has to be something to the method."

She let her eyes drift out of focus. I looked at my watch. After thirty seconds were up, she spoke again. "Okay," she said. "So Alfy Romero gave you his phone number and then forgot about you. Berlin's room was ransacked, and she hasn't been seen since. A girl with a shark tattoo like Berlin's was found in Dagger Bay, but the shark girl's been at the bottom of the bay for, like, months and Berlin only disappeared a week ago. Someone's calling you claiming to *be* you, and Sally Hansen's been menacing you for days. On top of all of this, Charlie—and everyone else—thinks you're a ho who hangs at clubs with the Stratford twins. *And* we still haven't found your purse."

My head spun. Just thinking about it all was enough to make me throw in the towel. Then the nameplate came to me again.

"Who do you think HATTIE is?" I wondered, doodling the name in cursive in my notebook.

Daisy furrowed her brow. "Maybe this Hattie person kidnapped Berlin from her room and dropped her necklace while she was trying to subdue her!"

I gave my friend a look. "If that's what happened, she's the dumbest kidnapper ever. What kind of idiot leaves behind a necklace with her own name on it at the scene of the crime?"

"Criminals always do that on *Batman*," Daisy said. "For instance, the Joker will rob a bank and leave behind a jack-in-the-box that says, 'Ha ha! The Joker strikes again!'"

I giggled. "The way things are going, I wouldn't be surprised if we *were* dealing with a Batman villain. Sally Hansen certainly dresses like one."

Daisy twisted her lip, thinking about something else. "One thing is really bothering me about all of this."

"Only *one* thing?"

"Well . . . what Genevieve said last night."

I sighed in exasperation.

"Are you *sure* you didn't sneak out and meet up with Alfy Romero?" Daisy asked.

I gave her a disappointed stare. "Daisy! You know me. I don't make out with boys—not even Alfy Romero—in public."

"Sorry. It's just that Genevieve and Charlie seemed pretty convinced."

"I know, and it's awful. Charlie's so mad at me. What a mess."

"Are you going to actually *talk* to him at some point?" Daisy asked.

"What am I supposed to say?" I protested.

She rolled her eyes. "You've only known each other, like, forever. I'm sure you'll think of something."

I would have asked her for some ideas, but we didn't have time to get into it. We'd arrived at our destination.

If you're ever in Halo City and in the market for a two-hundred-dollar T-shirt, I recommend that you stop by Rhonda B's. It's just about the most overpriced, useless store in the universe.

I can understand why Genevieve likes it so much. She's the type of girl who judges clothing based not on how it looks, but how much it costs. She sees some really ugly little skirt and thinks it must be great because it costs a month's rent. Not that Gen pays rent—but you know what I mean.

When we walked in, the manager on duty looked at me and Daisy with narrowed eyes. I guess it was clear to her that we're not gold card owners.

"Can I help you?" the girl asked coldly.

"Yeah," I said. "My friend Genevieve Reed was in here the other day, and she mentioned that Berlin Silver had been in recently."

At my mention of Genevieve's name, the manager's attitude changed. Suddenly I was important. "You're friends with Genevieve?" She fake-smiled. "Why didn't you say so?"

"I believe I just did," I stated.

The manager shifted in obvious discomfort.

"Genevieve and her brother were here about a week ago asking about Berlin. I hadn't seen her, but it turns out that my coworker, Helena, had. She waited on her a few days before that. Hold on a moment." The girl picked up a walkie-talkie off the counter and barked into it. "Helena, get out here for a second."

"Yes, mistress," came the put-out response.

As we waited, the manager stood at the counter, staring at the ceiling and drumming her carefully groomed nails on the counter-top. "I'm Jewel, by the way," she told me with a wan smile—the kind of smile that might as well have been a frown for all the warmth it conveyed.

"Charmed," I responded with an equally friendly smirk.

After a moment Helena appeared, stumbling into the room with a huge pile of sequined items in her arms. "What do you need, Jewel?" A few of the pieces fluttered to the floor. She tried to gather them up without fumbling the rest of the pile.

Helena was an enormous, bejeweled woman with caked-on foundation, fire-engine-red lipstick, and green eye shadow that looked likely to be Magic Marker. She must have been at least six-foot six.

"These customers are looking for Berlin Silver," Jewel said. "I told them that you'd seen her. And if those tube tops lose any of their sequins, it's coming out of your paycheck, so be more careful."

Helena looked up at us wide-eyed. She dumped the clothes that she was carrying onto the counter. "What do you know about Berlin?" she asked breathlessly, her voice a few octaves deeper than the hum of a lawn mower.

I took in Helena's broad frame, her thick fingers, her jutting Adam's apple. . . . I didn't know how I'd missed it before. Helena was a drag queen.

I eyed her warily, holding my cards close to the vest. I didn't want to divulge anything important until I knew more about this Helena character.

"We think she may have been murdered," Daisy said in a stage whisper.

I rolled my eyes. So much for strategy.

"What?!" Helena gasped. "No! That can't be!"

I gave her a rueful nod. What was I supposed to say?

Helena slumped down on a table full of clothes, carelessly knocking a pile of designer blouses to the floor. Jewel scurried over in exasperation and tried to gather them up. Helena covered her face with her huge hands.

"I've been so worried about her," Helena rasped. "I haven't heard from her lately, but I can't believe something like *that* could have happened."

"Well, we don't know for sure," I said quickly. I had to get this interview back on track. "How do you know Berlin, anyway?"

Helena sat up and tried to compose herself, prompting Jewel to stifle a tiny yelp as even more clothes flew helter-skelter.

"I need a hot dog," Helena said to no one in particular. She stood up and walked to the door, turning as she pushed it open. "Are you coming, girls?"

Daisy and I followed Helena, leaving a flabbergasted Jewel to mind the store by herself.

"Um, why are we going to get hot dogs?" I asked Helena as we followed her down the block.

"Because I can't stand to be in that dingy little store with that wench of a manager a moment longer," Helena told me. "Plus Bob's Dogs are the best in Halo City, and that's exactly what I need right now."

"You hear that Berlin Silver has been murdered and it makes you crave hot dogs?" Daisy asked incredulously.

"Berlin has not been murdered," Helena insisted. "I know her too well to believe a piece of nonsense like that."

When we reached the stand, Helena ordered three dogs, for which the vendor didn't bother to charge her. "Now," she said, "you girls tell me what you know."

"You first," I insisted. "How do *you* know Berlin?"

"Berlin was one of my best customers at the store," Helena said. "She was having trouble making friends her own age, so she and I became friends. Not good friends, but you know, *gal pals*." She sighed. "I thought of Berlin as a daughter, really. I gave her advice about boys, took her shopping on the weekends. Listened to her problems at school . . ." She paused, giving me a curious look. "What did you say *your* names were?"

"I'm Lulu," I said. "And this is Daisy."

"Lulu? Not Lulu Dark!" Helena exclaimed.

"Yes, that's me," I answered cautiously. "How do you know who I am?"

"Oh, Berlin told me all about you," Helena gushed. "She really admired you—and she was so happy that she'd made a real friend."

What? Berlin had told this woman that I was her friend? How weird. I'd barely known Berlin at all.

I didn't point that out to Helena, though.

"Anyway," Helena went on, "I'd been worried about Berlin for a while. She was a real mess the last time I saw her. She seemed upset about something, and she wouldn't tell me what. I was starting to think she might be in trouble. Then she came in Saturday before last acting like a complete crazy person. She barely talked to me, and she was looking for a whole new wardrobe. It was very strange."

Helena paused to take a bite of her dog. "When did you girls see her last?" she asked through a mouthful of food.

"Friday night before last," I answered. "But Genevieve Reed saw her a night after that. As far as I know, that was the last time *anyone* saw her."

"Oh, dear," Helena said. "What do you think could have happened?"

I gave her a knowing look.

"Now, listen here," Helena chided me. "I know that you think something terrible happened to Berlin, but I just don't see how that's possible. She'd never let anyone hurt her—she's too much of a little pit bull herself. Besides, who do you think could have done such a thing?"

I hadn't really thought about who, but when Helena asked the question, one name popped into my mind.

"Sally Hansen," I said gravely.

"Sally Hansen?" Helena asked. "I love her line of nail polish. It's chic yet affordable. But what does she have to do with Berlin?"

I gestured to Daisy. Dutifully she reached into her trench coat and pulled out my little Nikon digicam.

I turned it on and scanned through the saved photos until I found the picture of Sally Hansen I'd snapped the other day in the park. "Have you ever seen Berlin talking to this girl?" I asked, showing Helena the screen.

Helena thought hard, a long pink nail scratching her lower lip. "I don't think so," she finally said. "I'd remember a hot little number like that one."

"Whatever happened to Berlin, *she's* mixed up in it," I insisted, pointing to the screen.

Helena laughed raspy and low. "Not a chance. This little Hooters reject wouldn't be half a match for Berlin." She turned to the hot dog man, showing him my camera. "Ever seen this tartlet, Bob?"

He squinted as he examined the picture. "Can't say I have, Hel."

"Well, if I ever catch you selling her a hot dog, we're going to have problems. She's on my enemies list, and so is anyone who helps her out."

"Any enemy of yours is an enemy of mine," the vendor told her, then handed her another dog. "Here. It's on me."

"Thanks. And if you see Berlin, please tell her to call me! When you get to be a woman of my age, you worry."

Bob nodded and turned to his next customer.

"Come on, girls," Helena said. "I have an idea." She began to hail a cab, but I stopped her. We already had a car.

The drag queen was impressed by our classy wheels. "Now this is the ride I was born for," she said, climbing in with us. "I've got to get myself a rich boyfriend like yours, Lulu."

I let the comment slide. Charlie wasn't my boyfriend, but I felt dumb having to remind people of it every five minutes.

Helena directed the driver to an address on the west side, then explained that we were going to meet Francisco Jackson, a fashion designer who had been dating Berlin before she'd disappeared. Maybe he would know something about what had happened to her.

When Francisco Jackson opened his door to us, he was nothing like I imagined. When you think of fashion designers, you imagine them to be, well, fashionable. But Francisco was the biggest mess I'd ever seen. Even at his worst, Charlie at least showers and sprays on some deodorant. But at two in the afternoon on a Sunday, Francisco was still in his pajamas, hair a wreck, with at least three days of patchy stubble and a serious case of body odor. He was emaciated, pasty-faced, and blank-eyed.

This guy must be really, really *rich,* I thought. There's no other way that Berlin would ever date him.

"What do you want?" he growled.

Francisco clearly thought he was intimidating, but how scary is a man in a ratty bathrobe and fuzzy slippers? I knew in an instant that steely resolve was the only way to deal with this character.

Wordlessly I pushed my way past him into the apartment. Daisy and Helena followed close behind. I plopped myself down on the couch and crossed my ankles on the coffee table, which was piled high with old *Vogue*s and *W*'s.

"We want to know what's the what with Berlin Silver," I snapped. "And don't try to give us the runaround. We can make you talk if we need to. Daisy here has a brown belt in karate—and I have a black belt in ka-*razy*." I could get into this, I decided.

To my right, Helena stifled a laugh. I guess my steely side had taken her by surprise.

"Berlin? You want to know about Berlin?" Francisco snapped. "She's a monster, that's what's the what."

Helena and Daisy stared wide-eyed at Francisco, who began pacing the dark room. Back and forth, back and forth in jittery excitement. All the while he ran his fingers obsessively through his hair.

For a moment I considered the notion that I was wrong. Francisco *could* be intimidating. Not because he was physically strong, of course. But because something was off about him. Very off.

"Berlin Silver broke my heart!" he yelled, stalking toward me. "She ripped it out and stamped on it!"

I tried my best to remain calm. "Is that why you killed her?" I asked.

I was pressing my luck, but I didn't care. I had backup, and if I was going to solve this mystery, there was no time for pussyfooting around the big issues.

Francisco didn't even notice the accusation. He marched toward Daisy and Helena. "She tells me she loves me, tells me she wants to go to Las Vegas and get married. And I believe her. God! That's the last time I ever trust a woman." He paused, then whirled on me accusingly.

"You only lie when your lips are moving. You say you *love* someone, as in, *in love,* but what you really mean is that you want free clothes from the fall line and a seat next to Lil' Kim at the Jeremy Scott show. Well, I've had it. I'm never trusting anyone with a uterus again!"

He hunched over and clutched his belly in psychic pain. His body shook as he cried in big, silent heaves.

"So, um, are you saying that you haven't seen Berlin?" I ventured.

"Seen her?" He looked up at me from his crouch, his face puffy and wet. "Seen her!? I don't even know her number! She disconnected her cell phone, didn't tell me where she was going. She's the cruelest, most heartless person in the universe."

I ignored his histrionics.

"Okay, tough stuff," I said, my voice dripping with sarcasm. "If you hear anything from Berlin or remember anything about her, give me a call." I tore a page from my notebook and jotted down my number. He snatched it out of my hand and angrily crumpled it into a tiny ball, which he then shoved into the pocket of his ratty, plaid pajama pants. I looked at him pointedly and rolled my eyes in the most over-the-top manner possible. We left the apartment.

"Now I'm *really* worried," Helena said as we descended the dark staircase to the lobby. "I hate to say it, Lulu, but you may be right. That man did not inspire optimism."

"I thought you said Berlin was too tough to have been murdered," Daisy argued.

"Yeah, but Francisco Jackson is the sneaky type. The type that might have poisoned her drink or snuffed her out in her sleep."

Helena nibbled nervously on one of her fingernails. "I do not have a good feeling about this, girls; no, I don't."

I was feeling pretty unnerved myself. No doubt, Francisco was insane. Still, in some far corner of my brain there was a gnawing certainty that this just wasn't how it happened.

I dug into the pocket of my shorts and ran my fingers over the rough, jeweled surface of the necklace we'd found in Berlin's room. I had been carrying it with me since we'd found it.

Hattie, I thought. *Who is Hattie?* Since my tarot card reading, I'd become sure that the key to unraveling the mystery had something to do with her . . . whoever she was.

As we made our way to the limo, the possibilities were overwhelming me. Weren't mysteries supposed to get *less* complicated the more you investigated them? I thought the idea was to start with a bunch of suspects and narrow them down.

Instead this whole mess had begun with something simple—a stolen purse—and gotten more and more confusing as I'd gone along. No amount of Nancy Drew reading could have prepared me for this madness.

The driver opened the door and I slid into the leather seat that faced backward. I stared out the tinted window at the towering peak of the Halo Building. It's the tallest building in the city—the North Star on the Halo City skyline. As the car began rolling forward, from my seat the scenery was only receding. Soon it would disappear—along with my hope for finding out what *really* happened to Berlin Silver.

TEN SCHOOL ON MONDAY WAS PURE

torture. Chinese water torture, specifically, in the sense that it didn't seem that bad at first. But then it kept going and going and going— drip, drip, drip—endlessly wearing down my resolve with every passing second.

During history I considered messing with the teacher, which had never before failed to cheer me, but I didn't have the heart for it these days. All I could do was think about Berlin.

To add insult to injury, Charlie wasn't speaking to me. After the (fake) bombshell that Genevieve had dropped the other night, he decided that he would rather just hang out with his guy friends. Although I swore up and down that the rumors about me and Alfy were untrue, it didn't seem to make much difference to Charlie.

Daisy tried to perk me up at lunch with a constant stream of high jinks. She went all out; it was sweet of her to care. But even watching her toss strawberry Jell-O at the back of Blair Wright's white tennis skirt didn't do the trick. I tried to laugh, but it just came out a weak little gurgle.

How could I laugh when Berlin Silver was missing and no one seemed to care?

I couldn't wait to get out of school so I could continue my investigation.

Yes, okay. I called it an investigation.

Precalculus, my last class of the day, seemed to flip a switch in my mind. There's something intensely therapeutic about watching Mr. O'Neil scribbling on the blackboard, even if I have no freaking clue what any of it means. The lines and shapes and elegant, unintelligible formulas—it's all just dust on the slate. But to me, it's like performance poetry in another language, which makes it perfect for spacing out and thinking about my own crap.

Everyone with half a brain knows that higher math is pointless unless you want to be a math teacher, but math *class* is a different story. It's almost as good as those guided meditation tapes that Theo is always telling me I should listen to. You never know what part of your subconscious it's going to unlock.

I'm always surprised to look down at my notebook after precalc's over and see the doodles I've been unwittingly drawing—stuff I never even knew I had in me. Intricate, obsessive patterns; strange, otherworldly machines; mysterious faces . . .

That day Mr. O'Neil was talking about angles and arcs. Drawing wide curves on the board, scribbling like a madman. Sines and cosines and tangents. As he droned hypnotically, Berlin was dancing in my mind's eye, numbers and lines and triangles flying around her like reflections from a disco ball. In my daydream she was bouncing and shimmying in her distinctive sparkle tube top, tossing her hair, wilder and more carefree than she ever would have been in life, where she was always trying, and failing, to be cool. She was wearing dark sunglasses and whispering in a singsong voice, "Hattie, Hattie, Hattie is as Hattie does."

"Who is Hattie?" I wondered.

Tamika Danforth, who sits in front of me, turned around and looked at me like I should be committed. I was so gone that I was unaware I had actually said the words aloud.

Whatever. Tamika Danforth is the one who needs help. What kind of person actually pays attention in precalculus?

A second later I was back in my daydream, watching Berlin again. "Who is Hattie?" I asked her again, this time without moving my real-life lips. She didn't say anything, just smirked, unreadable behind her dark glasses. She jiggled and shimmied and reached into her tube top, pulling a manila folder from where there hadn't been one before. She handed me the folder and turned around with a sassy bounce, dancing off into the ether. BERLIN SILVER, the folder said.

Of course! The records! The ones we'd stolen from Mrs. Salmon—they were still sitting in my room! I hadn't even looked at them since the day we'd visited the Primrose attempting to find my purse. There had to be a clue in the folder.

I could have slapped myself for forgetting it. The old Lulu would have at least taken the time to peek at the grades.

As soon as class was over, I ran home as fast as I could, sad that Charlie's dad had called a halt to my limo service. I guess nothing good lasts forever. In my room I struggled to remember where Berlin's folder was hidden. Finally, after ten minutes of searching, I discovered the records under a huge pile of laundry. "Yes!" I shouted, even though no one was home. With a joyful pogo, I flopped onto my bed and opened the folder eagerly.

The first page in the file was Berlin's report card. There was only one set of grades from Orchard—from the January quarter. Amazingly enough, the marks were fairly decent—a few A's, mostly B's, and two scattershot C's, one of which was in gym and therefore didn't count.

With annoyance I realized that Berlin's GPA was, in fact, better than mine. I'd gotten *two* C's and a D—thanks in no small part to my fink of a Latin teacher.

I flipped the page to see Berlin's transcript from the rest of high school—before she'd transferred. *Whoa,* I thought. Orchard Academy had clearly done a good job with her. Before this semester all she'd scored were D's—not to mention the occasional F.

Adam Wahl was right about his ex, too. Berlin had attended five different schools before ours, including a boarding school in France. I could see why none of them wanted to keep her. Her disciplinary papers showed she was a real screwup.

I moved on to the medical records. I was hoping for a clue there, but it was pretty run-of-the-rich-girl-mill. I noticed that Berlin had severe allergies to shrimp and nuts. The well-bred always have that kind of thing. In case you're wondering, I have no allergies whatsoever.

Finally my eyes made their way to the bottom of the page. I let out a long laugh at the last note: *Unusually large third nipple.*

There was no question about it. Berlin was the product of upper-crust inbreeding. People make fun of West Virginians, but it's really the very wealthy who have the problem. They only marry other rich people, and eventually the gene pool's gotta dry up. Everyone's a cousin!

If Berlin had a baby with Charlie, they'd probably spawn a mutant child with three *legs*.

I turned the page and glanced at a photocopy of Berlin's driver's license. Yikes! It was a *horrible* picture; it barely even looked like her. She'd obviously gotten a nose job while she'd been in France and probably some collagen too. The old Berlin had thin, mean little lips and a honker that was long and pointy enough to stick in an electrical socket.

She would die if she knew I was looking at this, I thought, chuckling.

Then the guilt hit me. No, she wouldn't die—because she was already dead, and all I could do was laugh at her plastic surgery.

It was just so hard to think of Berlin as no longer living. Just over a week ago she'd been totally fine. Things changed so quickly that it didn't even seem real.

What a jerk I was. I *had* to find her killer now, if only to recoup all the karma I'd just tossed out the window.

With new resolve I found the emergency contact information for the Silver family. It was hard to make sense of it—there were phone numbers and addresses from all over the world—but I decided that the best bet would be to call the Silver compound in Motoropolis. I rolled onto my back and punched the number into my celly.

A voice answered after one ring. "Silver residence," a woman intoned mellifluously.

"I'm looking for——" I paused and glanced at the page next to me. "Babs Silver."

"I'm sorry, Mrs. Silver is not in town right now. Can I put you through to her voice mail?"

Thinking fast, I lowered my voice a notch and affected the nasal quality of all private school headmistresses. "This is Dr. Felicia Bober, at Orchard Academy," I said. "I need to speak with her about her daughter. Immediately."

"*I'm sorry,* Dr. Bober," the secretary said. "But you'll have to leave a message."

"That won't do," I told her. "It won't do at all. Berlin is in a world of trouble right now, and I'm afraid it can't wait. Mrs. Silver must have a cell phone where she can be reached."

There was a put-out sigh on the other end. "Just a moment," said the voice.

When I hung up, I had Mrs. Silver's number in hand and a smile on my face.

I am so good, I congratulated myself.

I dialed the number and dropped the Bober impression when I got Babs on the phone.

"Mrs. Silver? This is Lulu Dark. I'm a—well, I know Berlin. I need to talk to you about her."

"Oh, hello, Lulu," Mrs. Silver said. "I've heard so much about you. Berlin really admires you."

I held the phone away from me and stared at it. Once again, *Huh?*

Then I started feeling guilty as well. Weird as it seemed, Berlin had totally liked me, and I'd ignored her overtures at friendship like a total snob. It was sad to think that of everyone she'd met at Orchard, I was the one she considered herself closest to.

"What can I do for you, Lulu?" Mrs. Silver prompted.

At that moment I realized that I didn't even know what I was going to say. I couldn't tell her my real suspicions. Especially not over the phone. It would be too cruel.

"Um, have you heard from Berlin lately?" I asked, doing my best to sound unconcerned. "I haven't seen her in a week or so, and I was afraid she'd gotten sick or something. She hasn't answered her phone. I hope she's not mad at me."

There was a long silence. "You haven't seen her?"

"Not really," I murmured apologetically.

"Dammit," Babs snapped. Then: "Sorry, dear. I didn't mean to snap at you. It's just that's a bit of a pattern for Berlin. She seemed to be doing so well. But the school's been calling and calling about her, and I can't seem to get in touch with her either. What a nuisance. Can you meet me for lunch, by any chance?"

"Um," I said. "I'm in Halo City."

"I am too," Berlin's mom said airily. "Here on business. That's why I'm sure Berlin's hiding out. She'll do anything to avoid seeing me. So. Where can I meet you?"

After setting up a meeting with Mrs. Silver, I took a deep breath and bit the bullet. I needed Charlie's help, and I was willing to grovel if necessary.

"What do you want, Lulu?" he snapped when he answered his phone.

"Charlie." I sighed. "Please, please, *please* help me out here. I'm not going to apologize for lying about the other night because the fact is that I'm telling the truth. I did not, repeat *not,* ditch you to make out with Alfy. I'm sorry things have been so weird between us. I promise we can sort it out later, but right now I really need you to give me the benefit of the doubt."

"Why should I?" he asked peevishly.

"Why shouldn't you?" I retorted. "I have never lied to you, Charlie. Never. Why would I start now? Besides, if I *had* made out with Alfy, wouldn't I make sure to tell every jealous hag at Orchard Academy about it *personally?*"

There was a long pause.

"Fine," Charlie said sullenly. "What do you need?"

Charlie agreed to meet me and Mrs. Silver at Little Edie's. He still seemed unsure about the Alfy rumors, but he was starting to come around, and thank goodness. He'd be much better at talking to an aristocrat than I would. He was experienced with it from dealing with his own mother. And with what I had to tell Mrs. Silver, I needed all the help I could get.

·   ·   ·

When I got to the restaurant, I recognized Berlin's mom immediately. She was waiting at the table in the middle of the café, smoking a cigarette nervously. The tip-off was her jewelry—she had diamonds dripping from her neck and wrists and a huge tacky ring on her finger. Although she seemed to be trying for legitimacy, she was wearing a skimpy tank top and enormous Chanel goggles even though we were indoors. Her bronzed skin had that tight, stretched look that comes from serial face-lifts. It had to be her.

"Hi, Mrs. Silver," I said, approaching her. "I'm Lulu." I wanted to ask her to move to my usual table, since that's the place I'm most comfortable. But somehow it seemed rude.

Mrs. Silver glanced around the room before dropping her cig in an ashtray to shake my hand. "Hello, Lulu," she said. "I'm pleased to meet you."

We finished the handshake, then stared at each other blankly. I didn't know what to say next. I smiled nervously and took a seat. *Please let Charlie get here fast,* I prayed silently.

It was almost enough to give me religion that he chose that moment to walk in the door. And he was perfect. Seeing him in action is always such a surprise.

He's a total ruffian in day-to-day life, but when he's got to interact with someone like Babs Silver, Charlie completely transforms. He shook Bab's hand firmly, kissed her on the cheek with a smooth, "Mrs. Silver," and took a seat next to us. Yep, Charlie was a charmer. Babs melted like butter—and he didn't even let on that he was mad at me.

We ordered some appetizers, which Babs ate only at Charlie's behest. We talked small talk, or he did, rather, while I fretted about when to bring up Berlin. It took forever to work up the nerve, but finally I did it.

"Bab—I mean, Mrs. Silver," I stammered. "When was the last time you saw Berlin?"

Mrs. Silver placed her glass of wine on the table and exhaled a slow puff of smoke. I coughed loudly.

Mrs. Silver tsked. "Nasty habit," she said apologetically. She extinguished her cigarette. "I haven't seen Berlin since January. Since she started at Orchard Academy. But I keep in close contact. I'm sure you know that she can be a handful. She needs a lot of attention, so I talk to her at least once a week. When I can get ahold of her, that is."

It didn't seem occur to Mrs. Silver that perhaps Berlin was "a handful" because she'd been in boarding school since she was eight years old. I remembered my notebook entry from Saturday. Childbirth and insanity. There was *certainly* a medical connection.

"Have you spoken with her *this* week?" Charlie asked.

Babs gave him a smile. She was so impressed by him that she probably would have smiled if he'd sneezed in his hand and wiped it on her tailored wool pantsuit.

"Last time I spoke with her was two Fridays ago. She was on her way out the door. Something about going to see some handsome rock singer perform."

She no doubt meant the Many Handsomes' show. "But you haven't heard from her since?" I asked.

"Not a peep."

"Well, this might come as a bit of a shock to you," I said as gently as possible, "but Berlin hasn't been in school for more than a week."

Mrs. Silver sighed and rolled her eyes in frustration. "She always does this. She knew I was coming to town and just couldn't *bear* to see me. So she disappeared. This time she didn't even bother to call in and excuse herself from school. She always turns up eventually, but honestly, it's getting ridiculous. I'm beginning to think we should just bring her back to Motoropolis permanently."

Duh, I thought.

"Berlin had been acting strange for a while before she, um, disappeared," I said, parroting Helena's observation. Although I hadn't noticed it myself, I thought it was best to play along with Babs's notion that Berlin and I were tight. "Had you noticed that?"

"No, she seemed fine to me except for her sinuses," Mrs. Silver said. "They've been giving her trouble since January."

"Probably the surgery," I said unthinkingly. "I've heard it can do that."

Charlie's eyebrows shot up in alarm. He kicked me under the table, but it was too late.

Lulu Dark strikes again, I thought ruefully, *talking too fast for her brain to keep up.*

"Surgery?" Mrs. Silver seemed genuinely surprised, but I knew she was just covering.

I squirmed in my seat. "You know." I gestured to my nose, scissoring my fingers.

Mrs. Silver was suddenly angry. "We Silvers have *perfect* features," she said, pointing her own nose, which had obviously been under the knife as well, into the air. "She would never, ever get a nose job."

Charlie reached across the table, cutting in. "Absolutely," he said. "I guess Lulu just jumped to conclusions. A nose as beautiful as Berlin's doesn't usually come naturally in Halo City, that's all. But looking at yours, I can see where she gets it." He snuck a glance at me. *This is how it's done, you idiot,* his eyes telegraphed.

Berlin's mom seemed mollified. She placed a bony hand at her jawline. "Why, thank you," she cooed.

"The boys sure like it," I said, following Charlie's lead with more flattery. "Berlin has them lining up."

"I've been concerned about that, too," Babs said, still slightly wary. "Of course, I want her to be happy, but I want to make sure she's not dating the wrong types. God forbid she should get into trouble with some gold-digging ne'er-do-well. You know, she never dated much before. But now that she's in Halo City, she's gotten a little carried away."

Although I was learning a lot about Berlin's psychology, none of it was going to help me find her killer. I had one final thought before we called it a day. Maybe I could fit some of the pieces of this crazy jigsaw puzzle together. I pulled out my digital camera and found the picture of Sally Hansen.

"Have you ever seen this girl?" I asked, handing the camera to Mrs. Silver. She glanced down at it for a fraction of a second.

"No," she said, without much thought. "Is she a friend of Berlin's too?"

"I don't know," I admitted.

Babs slid the camera across the table. "Listen, I really appreciate your concern for my daughter, but I assure you Berlin has just taken another little sabbatical. She'll turn up eventually. She always does."

This woman was something else. The fact that her daughter had been missing for more than a week didn't even give her pause. If I were a truly terrible person, I would have told her that Berlin had been murdered, and I would have stomped out. Just to teach her what a bad mom she was. But I'm not a terrible person. I didn't even have the heart to broach the subject. And all of a sudden I felt even sadder for Berlin than before.

"Sorry to have wasted your time," I mumbled.

I took my camera and started to fidget with it while Babs and Charlie chatted about their summer homes. I was messing with the magnification, absently zooming in and out, in and out on Sally's picture when—

I gasped.

"Charlie," I said. "We need to go."

"What?"

I threw a wad of bills onto the table, knowing I was overpaying, and grabbed Charlie's hand, dragging him out of the café. Berlin's mother didn't seem surprised at our hasty exit. She just sat there, watching us go.

"Goodbye, Mrs. Silver!" Charlie called over his shoulder, waving in a panic. "Have an excellent stay in Halo City. See you again soon."

"When Berlin shows up, I want you two to go out together," Mrs. Silver shouted at Charlie as I flung open the door. "You would be *perfect* for each other."

"I can't believe you, Lulu," Charlie said when we were halfway down the block. "How could you be so rude? You really blew it."

"Charlie, you'll never believe it. That picture!" I exclaimed, making a beeline for the subway.

"What picture?"

"On my camera. Sally Hansen. *She* had my purse!"

"No way!" Charlie said.

"Yes! I didn't see it before because she had it over her shoulder. You could just see a tiny bit of it, peeking out from behind her skirt. But I know that was it! That pattern is unmistakable. And if Sally Hansen has my purse, there's only one person she could have gotten it from—Berlin!"

"What?" Charlie asked.

"Try to stay with me," I told him. "Your sister saw Berlin Silver with my handbag on Saturday night—the last time she was seen by anyone. This picture was taken the following Friday afternoon, *after* Berlin disappeared."

"Oh my God," Charlie gasped. "That means . . ."

"That means we've got to find Daisy. We have proof now. Sally Hansen killed Berlin Silv—"

I halted in my tracks. My face went white. Blocking our path on the sidewalk was none other than Sally Hansen herself. She had one hand on her hip and my beloved, familiar purse dangling from the other.

"Lulu Dark," she snarled. "I've finally caught you."

ELEVEN I STOOD, FROZEN IN

place. I knew I should run, but face-to-face with Sally, I found my Chinese slippers stuck to the sidewalk. Charlie was with me, I tried to console myself. At least I'd have company at the bottom of Dagger Bay.

Sally grunted and her arm came slashing toward me. I flinched. This was it! Something hit me hard in the chest. I looked down. My purse! It bounced off me and fell to the ground in front of my feet.

What was she, an ancient Egyptian? Did she want me to die with my belongings or something?

"Here's your hideous purse," Sally spat. "I hope you're happy with Alfy. He may be good-looking, but I think he traded brains with that bulldog of his somewhere along the line. And by the way, he cheats. As if you hadn't figured that one out already."

Wait a minute. What was she talking about? Wasn't this the part where she was supposed to kill me?

"Huh?" I wasn't yet ready to speak in full sentences.

"I found your purse in his apartment," Sally said. "So don't play dumb with me. I know you're Alfy's new hussy. Keep him; he's a troll. You'll find out for yourself once the novelty wears off."

Charlie's jaw dropped. "Lulu, I can't believe you," he mumbled.

I just stood there, trying to figure things out. But none of this made any sense.

"Sally, why have you been following me if you're not going to kill me?"

"First off, my name's not Sally, it's Lisa."

That's right. I had gotten so used to calling her by her nickname that I had forgotten it was only my invention.

"And *kill* you?" she said. "What are you smoking? Alfy's the one I want to kill. You're nothing to me but a dirty boyfriend thief. I just wanted to give you your purse back. And meet you face-to-face. It's all over town, so I don't know why I bothered, but still. It's called *closure*. Dr. Phil says it's important."

"Wait," I said quickly. "You've got it all wrong. I swear on a stack of . . . I don't know—phone books or something—that I haven't been messing with your boyfriend. Last time I saw him was that day at Halo Park, when you were spying on me."

She rolled her eyes. "I wasn't spying on *you*. I was spying on him. But you were flirting with him, and then I found your stupid bag in his apartment. With his phone number in it. I don't see why you're denying it. I tried to talk to you on the train the other day, but you wouldn't wait up. Where I come from, that's called being a coward."

Charlie cleared his throat. "Lulu, you swore up and down that you weren't lying to me."

"I'm not!" I defended myself. "If my purse was in Alfy's apartment,

I didn't leave it there because my purse was stolen the night of that concert."

Then it dawned on me. *Duh.*

"Berlin stole my purse," I explained. "*She* must have left it at Alfy's."

"Berlin?" Sally-slash-Lisa said. "Who on earth is Berlin?"

"Berlin Silver!" I argued. "The girl you killed and dumped in Dagger Bay!"

"I didn't kill anyone, you idiot!" Sally-slash-Lisa yelped. "Let alone some stranger named after a foreign capital."

"But if you didn't kill Berlin, then who . . . ?" I stopped short.

It was all coming together now. If Berlin had left my purse at Alfy's, that meant Alfy was the last one to see her alive.

It was so obvious. *Alfy Romero was the killer!* A murderous, cheating rock star!

I sighed. These things always turn out the same. Want to know whodunnit? It's the one who's fine as hell. How depressing.

"Come on, Charlie. I've figured it all out." I took his hand to run, but he wasn't budging.

"Not until you explain why you didn't tell me you were seeing Alfy Romero. Why did you have to lie about it?"

I hate it when everyone else is two steps behind me. I folded my arms across my chest, threw my hip to the side, and glared at him. "Charlie, *keep up.* I am not having a secret affair with Alfy Romero. Berlin Silver was. And he killed her!"

Charlie bit his lip, putting the pieces together for himself.

Now it was Lisa's turn to be freaked out. She glanced back and forth between me and Charlie. "You guys are lunatics," she said. She turned on her six-inch heels and hurried away. I couldn't believe I'd ever been scared of her.

"Come on, Charlie," I said. "We're going back to my place. Call Daisy and tell her to meet us. We need to hatch a plan."

"Wouldn't it make way more sense to call the *police* instead?"

"Nah. They didn't believe me last time and they're not going to now. That's okay. When I'm finished, they'll be on their knees thanking me. And there's no better feeling than being able to say, 'I told you so.'"

"What about sneezing?" Charlie said. "That feels really good. Or peeing after you've been holding it for an hour. Or—"

"Don't be so literal about everything," I cut him off. I definitely didn't want to know what was going to come out of his mouth next.

Back at the loft, we found Daisy was waiting for us on the front stoop. "Good job, gumshoe," she said, patting me on the back. For once I didn't argue about the moniker. Despite my instincts to the contrary, I was proud of myself for figuring things out.

We went to the kitchen. I cut up some Granny Smith apples, spread peanut butter on the slices, and took them to my room on a tray with three cans of Coke. It was a celebratory snack. The crime was solved; all that was left was the part where we confronted the murderer and tricked him into spilling everything.

If we could do it without being tied up and left for dead in the basement of a burning building with only our nail files and compacts as escape tools, I would consider it a job *very* well done.

Charlie, Daisy, and I lolled on my bed, nibbling the apples and brainstorming.

"We'll need disguises," Daisy said.

"Really? Why?" Charlie asked.

Daisy looked at him like he'd eaten a plate of stupid for breakfast. "If we're not wearing disguises, Alfy isn't going to confess anything. He'll know we're on to him and he'll just kill us too." She turned toward me. "Trust me. We need disguises. Disguises always make every plan better."

Charlie raised one eyebrow but didn't say anything.

"What should we be?" she mused. "Harem girls? I've got these great *Arabian Nights* pants that I haven't had a chance to use yet."

Charlie snorted.

"Um, Daisy, I don't see why Alfy Romero would confess his crime to two Halo City harem girls," I said.

Daisy wasn't deterred. "*Fiddler on the Roof?* We still have our outfits from the musical."

"How about something less, you know, *retarded*," Charlie suggested. Daisy scowled back at him.

"Charlie's sort of right," I broke the news gently. "I think that it will be more suspicious, not less, if we show up on Alfy's doorstep dressed like Cinderella and Snow White or Wilma Flintstone and Betty Rubble. It's the difference between a costume and a disguise. It's a subtle distinction, yet it exists."

Daisy didn't like what she was hearing. "Well, what's your suggestion, Shamus?"

"We don't need disguises at all. We'll have the cover of night to cloak us." I raised one eyebrow dramatically. "Let's just stake out Alfy's next concert, follow him home together, then force him to tell us the truth!"

"Fine," Daisy pouted. "The next concert is Thursday night."

"I'm in," Charlie volunteered. "This espionage thing sounds like fun."

I beamed at Charlie. "Sometimes I forget how great you are," I told him. I wrapped my arms around him and gave him a huge, wet kiss on the cheek. He just lay there, body stiff as a board.

Daisy smiled at me knowingly, and I remembered how Genevieve had accused me of leading him on. I quickly released Charlie, sat up, and scooted to the other side of the bed. "Right, um . . ." I said, clearing my throat. "So, yeah, we'll meet at the concert?"

"Thursday night," Charlie repeated.

I recovered myself and smiled my wickedest smile. "Thursday night. Friends, we have a date."

I found Charlie and Daisy at the entrance to the Purple Unicorn—a popular club in the Milliney District. We bought tickets to the Many Handsomes show and eased our way inside. Soon after, Alfy and the rest of the band took the stage.

With his dark eyes and ruffled hair, Alfy Romero looked as hot as ever. What a shame. For the second time I wondered why the bad guy always had to be such a fox.

Alfy's performance, however, was lackluster in comparison to the last one we'd attended. Maybe it was because I now knew there was something sinister about him.

Anyway, the band picked that night (of all nights) to do an extended set of encores. As the night wore on, Daisy began to feel nervous.

"You guys, I'm pushing curfew," she said, glancing at her watch. "If Svenska finds me out late, it's solitary confinement for sure."

"Don't worry," Charlie shouted above the band. "I'll stay."

Daisy gave Charlie a peck on the cheek. "Thanks!" Then she turned to me, all seriousness. "You must call me first thing tomorrow. First thing! I want to know everything that happens. Promise?"

As if I'd do anything else! I nodded and gave Daisy a hug before she made for the door.

Half an hour later, when Alfy announced "the last song of the night," Charlie and I slipped out. We walked around the club—to the back door in the alley—where we had a hunch Alfy would be exiting. Our instincts proved correct when he came sauntering out the door, still in his trademark T-shirt and torn jeans.

"Hide!" Charlie whispered. We ducked into the shadows and waited for him to pass.

A few seconds later the coast was clear. We both turned to see Alfy's silhouetted figure under the streetlamps, safe in the distance. We followed him in the darkness.

Alfy's sense of direction wasn't great.

Musicians, I thought. *They're so willy-nilly.* He wended his way through Halo City, taking his sweet time, hands jammed dreamily in his pockets and whistling one of his own songs. Guilt hadn't touched this killer. He was happy about something—probably his own satisfaction with his evil deeds.

There wasn't much to do while we trailed him. Charlie and I ambled along easily, letting the cool spring air seep in through our pores, chatting about not much of anything.

If there hadn't been a mystery at hand, it would have been nice. Then I felt this little burst of glee in my chest over the simple fact of me and Charlie walking side by side, just the two of us.

Maybe this was the time to clear the air about this whole Charlie-liking-me business. I was feeling bold and this seemed as good a situation as any.

"I guess we need to talk," I said.

"I guess so," he replied.

"Genevieve told me some things," I began.

"Yeah?" His tone was neutral.

"Yeah. And, well . . . I just want to say it would be a shame to ruin our friendship. But at the same time . . . I feel like . . . I don't know. I really missed you when you weren't talking to me."

He turned to me and gave me a shy smile. "Yeah, me too."

Charlie slid his hand into mine. For a second I was a little taken aback, and then I looked him in the eyes—they seemed bigger than ever. An unstoppable grin crept across my lips and I gave his hand a little squeeze. We kept walking, not saying anything, our arms swinging easy. I lifted my head up high and felt my back straighten. We walked in sync, our steps stretching a little farther than they did before.

The Halo City skyline was reaching up all around us—nearly brushing against the smooth edge of the moon. Every problem I'd encountered suddenly felt so small.

Yes, I thought, *I can do this now. I am the Princess of Swords.*

Finally, deep in the Butcher District, Alfy stopped. He was about a block ahead of us and from where I stood, he seemed to be searching his pockets for his keys.

"There!" I told Charlie. "That must be his place."

"Hurry!" he said, and we trotted ahead, trying not to look conspicuous. Meanwhile Alfy disappeared into the building.

"Great," I said. "What now?"

"Well, now we know where he lives," Charlie said. "We can come back tomorrow. Want to go to a diner and get something to eat?"

"Come on, Charles. Don't be such a slacker. We should stake the place out. We could see all sorts of suspicious things."

"A stakeout?" He perked up. I was appealing to his sense of adventure. He looked around, then smiled when his eyes landed on the Dumpster across the street.

"Oh no," I said, guessing his thoughts. "Charlie, I am not hiding in a Dumpster. That is so gross. There are probably rats and stuff in there. Not to mention annoying Dumpster divers."

"Dumpster divers are cool," Charlie said. "Live a little."

I sighed. There wasn't really anyplace else to hide, so I let him hoist me up into the pile of trash, praying that I wouldn't land on some scavenging-activist type.

Fortunately, this Dumpster was mostly full of construction garbage—Sheetrock, old boards, and stuff like that. Still, I was holding my nose prissily when Charlie jumped in and landed next to me.

"This is so cool," he said breathlessly. "I bet there's all kinds of good finds in here."

"Charlie!" I said. "Let's not kid ourselves here. You don't need this trash."

"No, but it's the principle," he said, hurt.

"Don't let me get in the way of your fantasies of poverty," I said.

We stood, peeking out over the edge of the Dumpster. Alfy's apartment stood there because, well, that's what buildings do.

"Okay," Charlie said, after we had been staring for ages. "Let's go get food now."

"Charlie," I said. "You are never going to accomplish anything if you don't improve your work ethic." I was talking big talk, but I had to admit that my back was starting to hurt.

"I guess we could sit down for a little bit, though," I finally decided. "We'll be able to hear if he comes out."

Charlie was almost mollified. He found a discarded, largely unstained foam mattress pad, which seemed suitable for sitting. I unclenched my fingers from my nose and found that the Dumpster didn't actually smell. I perched on the mattress pad. Charlie settled down next to me and we sat in silence for a minute. Eventually he leaned back, half reclining, and I did the same. Our eyes were trained on the sky, but somehow my hand found his again.

"So Charlie," I said as we were staring up at the stars, which were frankly pretty damn beautiful. "This is a romantic scene. Alone in the Dumpster together. Intrigue and suspense . . ."

I glanced over and saw him smirk puckishly. "What happens happens, right?" he said.

"I guess so." I shrugged. I raised my eyebrows hopefully. "So?"

Charlie gave me a brave look. He started to lean in and I felt that thrilling tingle up my spine again. I let my eyes close and tilted my head back. . . .

TWELVE SUDDENLY THERE WAS A

yell from across the street. "Lulu!" It was a man's voice. I bolted upright, leaving Charlie in the trash, lips still puckered, looking confused.

Across the street, on the sidewalk in front of Alfy's apartment, another romantic scene was taking place—between Alfy and . . . me!

Or rather someone who *looked* like me, canoodling in the doorway with him.

The girl's brown hair was the same as mine. So were her glasses, and she was wearing my trademark hot pink cowboy boots! I was chilled to the bone. "Charlie," I whispered urgently. "Look."

He pulled himself up to see what was going on. When he laid eyes on the girl across the street, who was now engaged in a hot and heavy smooching session with Alfy, he turned—stared at me—then turned back.

"Lulu, that's you!" he said.

"No, it's not. It's just a cheap copy. But why is Alfy Romero's girlfriend dressing up like me?"

We continued watching them in their slobbery embrace until they went inside. I was so pissed. Not only did I have a doppelganger, but *she* had to be the one starting all the rumors about me. I wasn't going to stand for it.

We sat back down again. Charlie struggled to make sense of what he had just seen. "Maybe it's some science-fiction thing," he guessed. "Like a clone or something?"

I gave an exasperated sigh. "Be real. I'm in more trouble than I thought, but I'm fairly certain there are no clones involved. Alfy and fake Lulu killed Berlin Silver, for whatever twisted reason, and now they're impersonating me. But why?"

"Maybe they're trying to frame you for the crime," Charlie ventured.

I had to admit, it was a plausible theory. "We have to stay awake until they come out again so that we can see where they go," I insisted.

"Whatever you say," Charlie replied, already yawning. He had stretched out on the mattress again and looked ready for a long nap.

Fine, I'd take the first shift.

I sat, kneeling by the edge of the Dumpster—gazing at Alfy's darkened building—waiting.

After a few minutes I could hear Charlie snoring next to me. He certainly had dropped off quickly. I wondered if he was annoyed about our interrupted kiss. From the look of things, he seemed not to care. He was curled in a tight little ball with his elbow shielding his eyes and his mouth hanging half open.

Like I said before, Charlie Reed is the most oblivious person I know.

I was awakened by the mid-morning sun pushing through my closed eyelids and what felt like a tin can jabbing into the small of my back. When I rolled over and opened my eyes, I saw Charlie lying next to me, still sound asleep.

I laughed. Here we were, sleeping side by side . . . in a Dumpster. Charlie would probably find it all very wild and romantic when he woke up, just like that time he and Lila Simmons snuck into the reptile house at the zoo.

It was still kind of hard to believe that we'd actually almost kissed. Close call!

Checking the clock on my cell phone, I was dismayed to realize that it was practically eleven in the morning. Fantastic. Not only had I had a terrible, stinky night's sleep, but I was sure I'd missed seeing fake Lulu leaving the apartment building.

I tried to be circumspect. At least I had learned of fake Lulu's existence, and although it didn't make sense yet, it was another important piece in the puzzle. I hadn't solved this mystery by a long shot, but some of the nagging loose ends were starting to tie themselves up.

For example, the wild rumors I'd been suffering through were obviously a product of this fake Lulu gallivanting around town. Perhaps she was even responsible for that strange phone call the other night. Whoever she was, she'd live to regret it.

"Charlie," I whispered, reaching over to shake him. He didn't budge, just let out another huge snore. "Charlie!" I said more urgently. I pinched him.

He eased his eyes open. "Hey," he croaked with a smile. "What's up?"

"Time to rise and shine," I said. "We need to get out of this Dumpster. It's disgusting."

"I'm going to nap a little longer," he said groggily. "You go on ahead."

"You can find your own way home?"

"Of course." He closed his eyes again and was instantly snoring.

Well. If he was enjoying his slumber, there was no reason for me to disturb it. For my part, I was getting out of this glorified trash can as quickly as possible.

I did a pathetic chin-up on the edge of the Dumpster and threw my leg over the side. I hung there for a minute, stuck, before I managed to pull my other leg up and swing over the side. Still off balance from sleep, I landed on my hands and knees on the asphalt below. This morning was not getting off to a good start.

And it was a school day—*the middle* of a school day, in fact. At least Dad was out of town, so I didn't need to steer clear of the apartment on my illegal day off.

I did a quick mental calculation and figured out that it was approximately fourth period at school. Daisy would be in study hall. I buzzed her.

"Hey, you little absentee," she answered after one ring. "What happened last night?"

I gave her the highlights of the evening, leaving out the part about almost kissing Charlie. She would find out about that in due time—and there were more important matters at hand.

"You have an impersonator!" she exclaimed. "That makes so much sense. I can't believe we didn't think of it before."

"Yeah," I said sarcastically. "It should have been like so obvious."

"What are you going to do now?"

"I'm not sure," I said. "I might just go home and take a nap."

"Don't do that," Daisy said breathlessly. "This is too exciting. I wish I had come with you last night. It sounds like it was crazy."

"That's one word for it," I told her. "But what else am I supposed to do? I don't know where to find fake Lulu."

"Let me come meet you," she said. "We'll figure it out from there."

"You're going to skip precalc?"

"Yeah, I'm so broken up over it. Whatever; Ms. Cook loves me. I compliment her outfit every day with these exact situations in mind. You know she'll let me bounce."

"Fine. I'll meet you at the Spier Avenue subway in twenty minutes," I said. "I'm so there."

Realizing I looked like death, I ducked into the bathroom of the nearest restaurant and attempted to spruce myself up. Unfortunately I was without my usual grooming products. But a little water and dispenser soap, along with some brown paper towels, are always enough in a pinch. Looking in the mirror, I decided that the best I'd be able to do was work the dirty, careless punk look. So I combed my fingers through my hair, washed my face, and adjusted the wayward bits of my outfit. It wasn't perfect, but it would have to do.

It's funny. I had been so spazzy for days, constantly fearful for my life, et cetera, but that morning, when I hung up with Daisy, I was feeling truly excellent. The sun was shining perkily, the birds were in full opera, and I couldn't stop smiling. I don't know what it was— maybe just the good weather and the bustle of the old-fashioned Butcher District streets—or the fact that I finally felt like I was making progress. Or a day off from school, a balmy morning. Or the idea that I was young and full of promise . . .

Okay, so maybe it was Charlie. I couldn't stop thinking about him. Every time I remembered that moment in the Dumpster—the moment where he was about to kiss me—I got a warm feeling all over. What was coming over me?

Suddenly I realized that without even knowing it, I was grinning madly. I did my best to stifle my smile, even going so far as to clap my hand over my mouth. After all, I didn't want people thinking I was some simpleminded tourist or something.

Things between us were still totally hazy, nothing had actually happened yet, and I still had my reservations, but despite everything I was on top of the world.

No one was going to kill me, I felt sure. Maybe they would try. But it wasn't going to happen. I was Lulu Dark. I was the Princess of Swords. Unstoppable.

I was still fighting my smile when I reached the subway. My stomach gave a growl. Daisy and I would have to go get something to eat before we did anything else. I took the stairs to the station two at a time, swiped my card, and walked to the edge of the platform to await Daisy's arrival.

I was standing there, back against a beam, whistling to myself and twirling a lock of hair around my pinky finger, when I felt a tap on my shoulder.

I turned to greet my friend. "Hey, Daisy, I——"

I stopped short. It wasn't Daisy standing in front of me. It was the anti-Lulu! She snarled and faced me head-on, wearing my very own sunglasses and pink cowboy boots. A Pucci scarf identical to the one I'd used over the weekend was tied in her brown hair. How had she found me? How much of her life did she waste following me?

I craned my neck, wildly searching for an exit route, or someone who could help me, but before I could do anything, the girl lunged toward me. She grabbed my wrists violently. I could feel her nails digging in.

My knees were shaking, but I knew better than to show my fear. "Get your hands off me, you cheap look-alike!" I yelped, trying to sound forceful as opposed to frightened.

"Save it," she hissed. It was the same voice as that of the mysterious phone caller. An imitation of my own. I struggled, pushing my arms, trying with all my strength to break free of her hold, but she only tightened her grip. "I *want* my purse back. Where is it?"

I studied her face, trying to divine the girl's true identity. It was familiar, but I couldn't place it. It was making me dizzy almost. Every time I thought I had honed in on a telltale detail, my head spun. It was like looking in a fun-house mirror.

My heart was thumping hard and I could feel the adrenaline coursing through me. I drew myself up and ditched the panic. "*Your* purse? You've got some freaked-out nerve. The purse is mine, has always been mine, and is safe and sound. Elsewhere. Now take off those glasses and tell me your name."

"My name is Lulu Dark," she snarled. I inched back, nearly banging my head on the beam behind me. Hearing her say my name with that demented, dead-serious set in her jaw—I caught myself almost thinking she was for real. A shiver ran down my spine. This poser truly believed she was me and *I* was the impostor!

"I am Lulu Dark," she repeated, like a mantra. "I am Lulu Dark."

"You're nothing like Lulu Dark," I growled. "For one thing, Lulu Dark is sane."

With that her face twisted so that she looked like an enraged gargoyle. In my wrists her talons seemed to grow an inch. I yelped in pain as I felt them break the skin, and she pulled me away from the metal beam, whirled me around, and shoved me to the precipice of the platform, where I teetered treacherously. The girl pushed her face close to mine.

"Listen up," she snapped. "You're going to take me to my purse right this second or you're going to be a pancake when the next train comes." She nudged me backward, and I felt myself wobbling.

I lifted my left foot and vigorously slammed the heel of my boot into her pink, copycat toe. "Ha!" I shouted as she fell backward, whimpering. With that I made a play for the exit. But before I could escape, she stuck out her leg and caught my foot mid-dash. I fell to the asphalt, arms stretched out in a face-first cement angel. I tried to scramble to my feet, but she was on top of me instantly, pinning me in a savvy wrestling hold.

"I warned you," she whispered in my ear. "Lulu Dark does not take crap from anyone, especially not a wannabe like you."

I shoved her off and kicked her in the ribs. I was at the wrong angle to do any real damage, though. She crawled toward me again, snarling and grimacing behind her dark glasses. I could hear the rumble of the subway in the distance, but I didn't have time to wait around for it to arrive. The rest of the platform was deserted. I had to get out of there.

I sprang to my feet and turned for the stairs again, but before I could move, scary Lulu grabbed my calf. With a quick, sharp yank she pulled me down. All at once we were blindly tearing and scratching at each other's faces and hair. Soon I started to run out of steam.

In a final burst of rage I gave a warbling battle cry. I swiped at her and snagged the fabric of her shirt. I ripped fiercely, tearing a chunk of her tight, baby blue oxford.

Then out of nowhere I heard a familiar yell.

"Hiiiii-ya!" There was a thump and fake Lulu's lips formed a stunned Kewpie *O*. The cavalry had arrived. Daisy had come to my rescue! I'd recognize the sound of her karate chop anywhere.

The doppelganger, who was still crouched on top of me, twisted around. Daisy towered over us, standing proud like a superhero. "How about picking on someone with a brown belt?" she asked sweetly.

That was enough for Dark Lulu. She jumped up, cautiously backing away from us. I stared hard at her and noticed a strange mark near her hip bone—right where I'd torn her shirt. I looked closer and gasped. It was a tattoo. A silver shark!

Wide-eyed, I pointed and opened my mouth, but before I could speak, the anti-Lulu swung around and leapt for the turnstile.

Daisy helped me to my feet. We raced up the subway stairs after the tattooed faker—but it was too late. She had disappeared.

"So close!" Daisy moaned. "We almost had her."

"Daisy," I said, still gasping for breath. "That was . . . I mean . . . Fake Lulu—she's not just any girl."

"I can see that," Daisy said impatiently. "She's freakishly strong. She should join the carnival."

"I mean." I was stumbling over my own words. I could barely believe what I was about to say. "I mean, *that* was Berlin Silver. She's alive!"

THIRTEEN IN A DAZE WE MADE

our way to the nearby Halo City Public Library. Mostly I was looking for some peace and quiet; someplace where I could recalibrate my out-of-whack mental compass.

Daisy and I made our way to a reading room. Unfortunately, my mind simply wouldn't rest. There were too many questions clanging around in it.

For instance, was that girl in the subway really Berlin? My brain insisted that she was. But if so, why was she dressing like me?

My brain also insisted that Berlin Silver was dead. But how could that be when she had just tried to push me in the way of an oncoming train?

Finally, who was the shark girl the police found in the bay? Why did she and Berlin have the same tattoo? How were the two of them connected?

After about five minutes of sitting in silence, I didn't feel any more decompressed than before. I stood. "I'm itching for more information," I said. "Let's see if we can dig anything up on Berlin."

"Let's start with the shark girl article," Daisy said. "You know. The one that made you think Berlin was dead in the first place."

"Might as well," I said. I gave a resigned sigh. "That's what Nancy would do, right?"

Daisy threw an arm around me. "Come on, super-sleuth. Let's find a computer."

It wasn't a challenge to locate a free one. Even in the main room at the Halo City library, they seemed to understand that the age of Gutenberg was long gone. Now it was the age of Microsoft, and what the cavernous room lacked in printed tomes, it made up for in computer terminals.

We pulled two chairs up to the nearest screen and called forth the newspaper database. HALO CITY SHARK GIRL, I typed, hitting the enter key with a bang. To my surprise not one but two articles appeared on the monitor—one from a week ago and one from that very morning.

SHARK GIRL AUTOPSY REVEALS DETAILS, the more recent headline declared. I clicked to see the whole article. Daisy leaned in to study it with me, and we hadn't even read past the lead paragraph before my mouth dropped open in thunderstruck amazement.

The office of the Halo City coroner announced this morning that the identity of the mysterious "shark girl," whose body was discovered last Friday in Dagger Bay, is now known. Officials are not yet releasing the name of the deceased, and the cause of death remains unknown. Forensic evidence, however, conclusively proves that the body had been in the bay since late December or early January before it was snared last week in the wayward net of a shrimp barge.

The rest of the article mostly recapped the origin of the story and described the tattoo found on the body. But I only skimmed it anyway. My brain was already whirring, trying to piece the information together.

"So Berlin's been alive all this time," Daisy said when she was done. "Charlie was right. The tattoo *was* a coincidence."

I tapped my chin, considering. "I'm not so sure," I said.

"What?" Daisy shook her head in disbelief. "How can you not be sure? You told me it was Berlin who attacked you in the subway. And it says right here that the shark girl can't possibly be her."

I couldn't explain it, but something was nagging me—insisting that there was more here than met the eye. But what, exactly? What was everyone missing? I needed some time to think it through.

"Let's go to Macaroni's," I said. "My treat. I'll explain everything then."

We made the walk to the restaurant, which was six blocks away, in silence. As we strolled, I twisted all my facts and hunches together in every combination, like a Rubik's Cube, lining up all the elements into an answer that made sense.

Daisy was having a hard time being patient by the time we were seated at Macaroni's. "Come on, Lulu," she begged. "Quit keeping me in suspense! This is worse than waiting to get my grades on report card day."

"Just hold your horses till the food comes," I told her. "I need your help hammering everything out."

At least we didn't have to hem and haw over what to order. They only serve two things at Macaroni's and, luckily, they happen to be the two most delicious menu items in Halo City—homemade macaroni and cheese and chocolate milk shakes. Once you eat mac 'n' cheese at Macaroni's, you'll never go back to the neon orange box kind.

When the food finally came, I dug in with gusto. I hadn't eaten anything since dinner the night before. I polished off the plate in three minutes flat. Then I grabbed my milk shake and took a long, languid sip. It was delicious.

Finally, stomach satisfied, I whipped out my notebook. "Okay," I told Daisy. "Let's figure this out. I think we've got all the information we need."

"I don't see how," Daisy said. "Especially when you consider the shark girl. Lulu, she died four months ago. It can't have been Berlin. We've been going to school with her since January."

"January," I said. "Exactly."

"What do you mean?"

"The shark girl died in January. Right before we met Berlin."

"Okaaay." Daisy still wasn't following.

"The girl we saw today was the girl we've been going to school with. The girl we *thought* was Berlin. She and the girl in the river had the same tattoo." I paused, letting the information sink in.

"So?" Daisy asked.

"So the girl we thought was Berlin is an impostor. She's been impersonating Berlin since January, when she killed her and took her place."

Daisy's face was blank with utter shock. She dropped her fork to her plate. "How can that be?"

"Add it up. 'Berlin' hasn't seen her mom in months. She's been avoiding her. She's only talked to her on the phone, and even then Mrs. Silver said she sounded different. She chalked it up to sinuses, but she must have been wrong. And get this. The picture on Berlin's driver's license—the one in her file—it didn't even look like her. I assumed she'd just gotten a nose job, but her mom swore she hadn't. Now it all makes sense. All this time we thought we knew Berlin Silver—but it's been someone completely different passing herself off."

Daisy rubbed her forehead, taking it all in. "But why?"

"That's the real question. Who and why?" I paused to think about it. "Berlin Silver isn't a bad person to be. For one thing, I'm sure her parents give her tons of money. She can buy anything she wants. Whoever is impersonating her could have wanted her allowance."

"Lulu, this is unbelievable," Daisy said.

"I know," I said. "But it's the only explanation that makes sense."

A look of worry crossed Daisy's face. "Let's say you're right. This twisted impostor is impersonating *you* now. What if she wants *you* out of the way?"

"It's possible." I nodded. "But you know, the really freaky part about all this is that I don't think she realizes she's *impersonating* me. On the train platform she really thought that she was me and that I was the impersonator."

"If that's true, it only makes her scarier," Daisy warned. "The worst thing about crazy people is how unpredictable they are. Just look at my mom!"

"You're right," I decided. "We need to find this impersonator and stop her before she decides that there's not room enough for two Lulus in Halo City."

"Which brings us to our next question," Daisy said. "If the impersonator isn't Berlin Silver, who is she?"

I had an idea about that too. I dug my hand into my pocket and retrieved the nameplate necklace. I slapped it on the table. The overhead light bounced off it. We both looked down and stared. It just lay there, practically screaming.

I put pen to paper and wrote it down. *Fake Lulu = fake Berlin = SOMEONE NAMED HATTIE.*

FOURTEEN DAISY HAD TO

be at Little Edie's for the afternoon shift, and I was undecided about my next move, so I headed back to the apartment. The first thing I did was Google the name Hattie, which, of course, pulled up only a candle maker in New Jersey and a bunch of genealogy charts from colonial times. I tried a few other combinations: Berlin Silver = Hattie, Hattie Berlin, Berlin Hattie, Berlin Hattie Silver. Nothing. Now I was stuck—all I could do was hope something would come to me.

So far, revelations had appeared at exactly the right moment, from out of nowhere. Marisol's mom had been right. I needed my friends, but when push came to shove, real answers came from within.

I thought about the way Hattie had demanded that I give her back my purse while we were struggling on the train platform. I looked over at my trusty old bag, sitting where I'd left it on the corner of my desk.

I'd gone through the purse the day Sally-slash-Lisa returned it to me, so I already knew that everything I'd lost was still inside. I dumped the contents out on my bed. My ID, an old tube of lipstick, receipts, scribbled unintelligible notes, photo booth pictures of me with Daisy and Charlie. A snapshot of my mom and dad, when they were young and stunning. Nothing all that interesting, really, but all of it was suddenly more precious than ever. I took an old, smudged sales slip from the bodega down the street (*toilet ppr/.99, cffee flters/2.99*) and clasped it to my bosom sentimentally. "I've missed you, old receipts," I said aloud, not caring that it's crazy to talk to yourself.

I gave the empty purse one last shake and found that it didn't quite feel empty. I shook it again more vigorously. Nothing else came out, but when I listened carefully, I could hear a faint jingling sound. I turned the purse over and searched the inside. That's when I noticed something new—a small tear in the lining. I opened the mouth of the purse a little wider and fished around in the hole. I grasped something hard and slightly sharp. I pulled it out of the lining and held it up to the light. A key!

It was small and dull and silver colored, hanging on a no-nonsense dog tag key chain. Engraved on the chain was a brief legend in fancy script: *The Barbara. 349.*

The key obviously belonged to the Barbara Hotel—the most famous flophouse in Halo City. It had long been a refuge of the down-and-out and glamorous. It clicked immediately that a wannabe like Hattie-slash-Berlin would have been attracted to it.

All sorts of messed-up stuff had happened at that place, but it was all messed up in the most stylish way possible—with legendarily troubled celebrities involved. It was where Judith Johnson, famous actress of the 1960s, had died of an overdose on painkillers and where Claudia Fujitsu had stabbed her husband, the punk god Alan Evil, in the seventies. In the eighties Pinky Bernstein, the seminal performance artist, had gotten busted for running a large-scale counterfeiting operation from the penthouse—claiming it was all in the name of art.

And those were just the highlights. The list went on and on. True, not much had happened at the Barbara since Pinky's capture, but maybe Hattie wanted to be the hotel's next notorious tenant.

It was a brand-new lead, and a promising one at that. I had to get to the Barbara ASAP!

Since Daisy was working, I called Charlie. I punched in the number, my stomach fluttering and my mind zooming off in every direction. I clutched the hotel key tightly as the phone rang . . . and rang.

Where was that boy? I knew I couldn't wait; I was going to have to go it alone.

I took a metal spatula from the kitchen to use as a weapon, just in case. After my pathetic encounter with Genevieve, I'd decided that I wasn't ready for a knife fight. Until then I'd have to settle for less-lethal kitchen implements.

I hurried to the Barbara Hotel, which wasn't a long walk from my house. The weather was still nice, but evening was approaching, and the sky had taken on a different, more violent character. It was a jarring shade of pink, with dark purple clouds.

If it had been a different situation, it would have been a stunningly gorgeous sunset. But walking past the warehouses and chop shops that lie on the edge of that neighborhood near the hotel, I knew the sky was telling me to watch my step.

The streets were deserted and I brandished the spatula, ready to swat at anything that dared to cross me.

The Barbara Hotel is right on Dagger Bay. It's tall and majestic in its own dilapidated way, and it appears to rise right up out of the water. It's one of the oldest hotels in Halo City, and you can tell. Ivy crawls up the red brick facade, and the stone lions that guard the entrance are cracked and eroding. The windows are all frosted over with dirt, and that day there didn't seem to be a light shining from any of them.

Still, the outside of the place is positively deluxe compared with the inside, which, I quickly found out, is plain old gross.

I walked through the old-fashioned wooden doors. The lobby of the landmark building looked like the waiting room of an auto repair shop—all spazzy fluorescent lighting and gray wall-to-wall carpet. The only furniture was some cheap, undistinguished chairs and a fiberboard end table with three-year-old copies of *Modern Golf* magazine sitting on it.

There was no one behind the reception desk, so I pushed the button for the elevator.

When the elevator descended, I found that it was the ancient kind, where you actually have to pull the door open and there's no comforting *ding* at each floor. Instead all I could hear was creaking and wheezing as it pulled me upward, suspended, I guessed, by a piece of twine or a broken cable repaired with a shoelace. One of the two lights inside the tiny lift was burned out, and my reflection in the greasy, graffiti'd mirror was cast in harsh shadows. I jangled the room key in the palm of my left hand, still clutching the spatula tightly in my right.

I was only going to the third floor, but it took forever, with the mechanism stopping and starting jerkily along the way. Every time it lurched, I expected to plunge to the ground. I pictured myself landing in the basement, a bloody, broken heap, while Hattie stood at the top of the shaft, holding a pair of wire cutters and cackling.

When the elevator finally stopped on the third floor, I pushed open the rusty door and stepped out into a spooky, darkened hallway. I picked a direction at random, scrutinizing the numbers on every room, trying to figure out if I was headed the right way. It should have been an easy task, but the place was like a maze, with a corner every five feet and mysterious dead ends everywhere. There was no sound. Only my shoes padding against the stained carpet and my heart pounding hard against my chest.

A weird noise echoed through the stillness. It was a distorted, high-pitched warble, like the voice of a withered, shrill old hag. She was repeating the same phrase over and over. "Very soon but not yet! Very soon but not yet!" After about the fifteenth time I realized that the sound was coming from a parrot. Probably another resident's pet.

I wandered farther into the labyrinth of the hotel. Finally I came to Hattie's room—number 349. Summoning my courage, I took a deep breath and banged on the door. If she answered, I decided, I'd just whack her with my spatula until she had no choice but to surrender.

Luckily I heard no response. I slid the key into the lock and slowly turned the knob, holding my breath as I eased into the room.

It was pitch black when I entered. I flipped the switch on the wall to find that the ceiling light was burned out. "Hello?" I called, crossing my fingers that there would be no answer.

"Very soon but not yet!" the parrot cried faintly in the distance. I slammed the door behind me, shutting out the sound of that creepy bird.

I groped my way around the room and finally felt a desk. Searching with my hands, I discovered a lamp and flicked it on.

When I saw what I was facing, my spatula clattered to the ground. I had to grab the desk chair for support.

The wall directly in front of me was plastered with photos. Photos of *my face*. Hattie had painstakingly constructed a disturbing collage devoted to me!

When I had calmed down enough to inspect the collection further, I recognized yearbook photos, magazine shots of me and my mom at her premieres, a postcard of a portrait my dad painted of me brushing my teeth, and even a clip from the *Halo Reader* of me as a toddler sitting on Santa's lap. How had she found all this stuff? I hadn't even known that most of these pictures existed.

But there was more. Three-by-five snapshots that Hattie must have taken in public. Me buying a pretzel on the street. Me coming out of my apartment with keys in hand. Me walking out of the subway, standing in line outside the movie theater with Daisy, eating at an outdoor café. Most of the pictures had been taken in the month before my purse had been stolen.

Hattie was spying on me all that time!

The longer I stood there examining Hattie's psychotic photo shrine, the more my breath quickened. A thin sheen of perspiration formed above my lip and along my brow. I felt like I was going to be sick. In an attempt to calm myself, I sat down on the bed, facing the other way.

No! I clapped a hand over my mouth to keep from screaming.

On the opposite wall, scrawled in a red substance that could only be blood, was the same phrase written over and over again in a messy, off-balance scrawl.

LULU DARK CAN SEE THROUGH WALLS. LULU DARK CAN SEE THROUGH WALLS. LULU DARK CAN SEE THROUGH WALLS.

FIFTEEN

scrawl and realized, with some degree of relief, that the "blood" was actually lipstick (Dior Fiery Red—somehow Hattie knew that it was one of my favorite shades).

But what could the phrase mean?

I stared at the wall, frozen in place. I closed my eyes and breathed deeply until the danger of a youthful heart attack seemed to subside. Then I remembered the night everything started—the night of the first Many Handsomes show.

"Lulu Dark can see through walls, you know," Charlie had joked to fake Berlin. Obviously it had had some significance to her, but it was hard to think why.

I knew I had to get out of that room fast, but I wasn't leaving until I found all the evidence I could. I just hoped I'd already seen the worst of it.

I walked over to the desk. On top I found a stack of letters, all addressed to Hattie Marshall, all unopened.

So I was right, I thought, with a fleeting sense of satisfaction.

Hattie *was* our girl's name. The return address was for someone named Susan Marshall, in Motoropolis.

Who was Susan? Hattie's mother? I didn't have time to pore over the letters just then, so I grabbed them and dropped them into my trusty purse. There would be plenty of opportunity to read them when I was safe and sound at home.

Next I pulled open the top drawer of the desk to find a sheaf of papers. It was "Berlin's" schoolwork, arranged in chronological order from the beginning of the semester. The stuff on top of the pile—the oldest stuff—was presentable and thoroughly completed. She'd gotten A's and B's on most of it. But as I flipped through the papers, toward the work from March and April, the handwriting began to break down, from a neat, almost anal-retentive script to a furiously scribbled, error-ridden chicken scratch. Every other word was crossed out with thick, jagged lines. The grades were C's and D's, mostly—with some F's.

At the bottom of the pile was her Future Career Day paper. She'd never turned it in, and it didn't have a name on it at all. It looked like it had been written by a five-year-old after a forty-eight-hour sugar binge. I read it carefully.

IN THE FUTURE I WILL BE A STAR

My future career is to be a star. I don't know if it is going to be in movies or a singer or a supermodel or be on reality television or marry someone famous or what, but everyone in the world is going to know my name. And they will stare at me when I walk down the street and ask for my autograph and they will think that I am so beautiful.

What I am doing to become a star is I am having new friends and buying clothes. And I am stopping all the ugly things I used to do that make me seem gross and unpopular. (a) Eating paper, (b) going to illegal cockfights, (c) falling asleep during the news every night are some of those things. Also (d) having an ugly name and not a glamorous one.

It is important for people to know that you are important and special and that is why you have to be friends with rich people or people who are pretty or people who are on MTV if you can't be on it yourself. Today, for my Future Career Day activity, I became friends with Millie Stratford, who is always in the newspaper, and I made out (again!) with Alfy Romero, who I think is going to be my boyfriend now. He is kind of a rock star and he will be very famous soon even if he is just sort of famous now.

My goals for the next month are to (a) go to lots of parties with the Stratford twins, (b) make out some more with Alfy, and (c) get my picture in the gossip page many many times by being real hyper at the parties. My goal after that is to be on the Halo City's Best-Dressed list. But if it has to be worst dressed that is okay too because it is something.

In conclusion, my future career is star. I am working

very hard toward this goal. I am so glad I found the purse
because it is really helping me be my true famous self.

"Wow," I said aloud when I was done reading. "That's really pathetic."
The "paper" was especially strange because it was, well, stupid. And
based on her other work, not to mention my interactions with her at
school, Hattie, or whatever you want to call her, certainly didn't
seem stupid. In fact, she had to be pretty smart to pull off all the
crazy tricks that she'd managed.

The other unusual thing about it was that it was the only thing I
could find in which Hattie didn't seem to be pretending to be another
person.

Maybe it wasn't stupidity but craziness that made the paper so
childlike, I hypothesized. Yes, impersonating someone is crazy to
begin with, but to do it for four months is probably enough to make
a person completely lose it.

I put the paper in my purse with the rest of the evidence. Then on
a hunch I dialed the front desk. "Hi," I said when the clerk picked up,
"this is . . ." I paused. What name had Hattie used when she checked
in? I wondered.

After a beat I decided, based mostly on the mail, that this was the
one place where she could be herself. Her secret hideout—her Bat
Cave—where she went when being someone else was just too much.

"This is Hattie Marshall in room 349. Have there been any messages for me?"

"I'll connect you to your voice mail," the clerk said.

Yes! My instincts were correct. I was on fire.

There was a click, and the robot voice mail lady was on the line. "You have. Seventy-five. Messages," she said in her familiar monotone.

The words gave me a serious jolt. Seventy-five messages? Hattie must not have checked them since she'd arrived in Halo City.

I listened to nearly every voice mail. They were all from the same person. Susan Marshall. The one who sent Hattie all those letters.

Susan, it seemed, was Hattie's older sister. Her first few voice mails were angry; something about stealing a hundred dollars. But as they went on, Susan was starting to panic.

"Hattie," she said in the last message, "forget the hundred dollars you took. It's okay—you can have more if you need it. I just want to know you're okay and take you home to Motoropolis. Hattie, I'm coming to Halo City on Monday. I'll be staying with Cousin Rhonda. Call me. Please."

As she gave the number, I scratched it down in my notebook. Susan and I had a few things we needed to discuss.

Susan met me at Little Edie's, which I was beginning to think of as my office as well as my hangout. Daisy was there too, ready to defend me if Susan was as nutty as her sister. Once I saw Susan, however, I knew my fears were unfounded.

Susan Marshall was about thirty, I guessed, but she looked like the kind of person who had lived through a lot. You could tell she had once been beautiful—in fact, she looked quite a bit like Hattie—but years of stress had taken their toll. Her face was careworn, aged with worry lines. Her hair was streaked with gray, and she was shaped sort of like a potato. Susan's outfit consisted of black stirrup stretch pants, white Nike high-tops, and an electric blue tunic tied around the waist with a gold lasso belt. Some people might have described it as tacky, but even with her enormous, permed hair and dangly price tag earrings, I thought she looked kind of cool.

"It all sounds like Hattie." Susan sighed after I related everything I'd learned. (Actually, not everything. I left out the part about the murder.)

"I'm sorry to be the one to tell you all this," I responded, meaning it. "But I figured, the way Hattie's been acting lately, she needs help."

Susan nodded. "Ever since she graduated from high school, she's had such problems."

Her last sentence stopped me cold.

"What do you mean, *graduated* from high school?" I asked.

"Hattie is twenty-two years old," Susan told me. "But she was so popular in high school, and she's always wanted to just go back to that. I'm not surprised that she found a way to actually make it happen. We grew up on the wrong side of the tracks, you know. Never had much money, although we made do. Mom kicked Hattie out of the house the day she graduated, and Hattie never really recovered. After that it was just one thing after another. Fighting, stealing money. And stealing clothes, of course. She was always wanting more clothes—and designer ones. She could never pay for them. Four hundred dollars for a T-shirt. To me, that's just dumb.

"Not for Hattie, though. She was so obsessed with being someone different, with being someone that she thought was better. To her, that meant rich and famous. She read all those magazines, saw those pictures, and thought that the only thing that would make her happy was if she could be on the cover herself. Do you know she sent seven videocassettes to MTV? She wanted to be on that, whatchamacallit, that *Real World* so bad. Seven tapes!"

"That's ludicrous," I said. Daisy kicked me under the table. She knew I couldn't wait till I was eighteen so I could try out for *The Real World* myself.

"When she disappeared, I was angry at first," Susan went on. "I'd been letting her stay with me, and then she just up and leaves. No thank you or anything, and all of my cash in her back pocket. She sent me a postcard a few weeks later, telling me she was safe, and that's the only way I even figured out she was staying in that weird hotel. I went there as soon as I got to the city, but she wasn't around. She never answered any of my letters or phone calls. I was sure something awful had happened to her. Thank goodness she's fine."

Daisy sat there, absorbing everything. I could tell she was still having a hard time believing all of this.

"You wouldn't happen to have a picture of your sister, would you?" I asked.

"Well, of course," Susan answered. She fished her wallet out of her bag and handed us a crisp two-by-three photo.

Daisy peered down at it. A look of recognition crossed her face. "You were right, Lulu," she admitted. "You were right all along."

She handed the picture to me. It showed a young-looking girl in a white, oversized sweatshirt and light blue high-waisted jeans. The sweatshirt read SUPERSTAR in cheesy airbrushed script. Her hair was frizzy, and her makeup was straight up garish—all the wrong colors in all the wrong places for her bone structure and complexion.

But her face . . . this girl was undeniably the person I had known as Berlin Silver. The person I now knew as Hattie.

There was no more beating around the bush. I had to tell Susan the truth. I braced myself, took a swig of coffee for courage, and spoke. "Susan," I said gently. "I have to tell you something."

"Yeah?"

"You know how I told you that Hattie was impersonating a rich girl named Berlin Silver?"

"Yeah." She folded her arms across her chest and cocked her head, waiting to see what I was going to say next.

"Well," I said. "They found Berlin's body in Dagger Bay. She's been there for four months. I think Hattie killed her and stole her stuff so that she could take her place."

Susan shook her head. "No way. That's crazy. My sister might be a little messed up, but she'd never hurt anyone." She paused, then corrected herself. "Well, she might give someone a black eye. Actually, she's given a few people black eyes. And a few bloody lips here and there. But that's it. She's just emotional. And she'd never kill anyone."

Although I was touched by Susan's faith in her sister, it was obvious that she was deluded. After all, Hattie had been ready to shove me onto the train tracks.

I decided to play along with her for the time being, but I wasn't

going to let this lady talk me into thinking Hattie was just some mis-
guided soul with a heart of gold.

Underestimating your enemy is always the biggest mistake.

"Well," I said, "maybe you're right. But either way, we have to find
Hattie and stop her."

"You're right. We have to. For her own good," Susan said quickly.

"And yours," Daisy muttered under her breath.

Luckily I had a pretty good idea of where we could find her.

"Come on," I said, "let's get out of here. I've got a plan."

SIXTEEN It was midnight, and

I was poised on the edge of the couch in the stark, dimly lit apartment that Hattie had been sharing with Alfy Romero.

The place was all sleek and soulless and modern. Even if I hadn't been sitting there waiting for my clone to show, it would have given me goose bumps. Everything at Alfy's was glass and chrome and leather. It was the kind of place that Dr. Evil would find cozy.

I shifted slightly in my seat. An industrial-looking clock on the wall ticked out the passing seconds. My leg twitched in my cowboy boot, anticipating Hattie's arrival.

Now is not the time for nerves to get the better of you, I scolded myself. I put a hand on my knee to still the shaking and let my gaze wander around the room.

This certainly isn't how I expected to make it into Alfy's place, I thought. But then again, nothing was going the way I expected it to lately. I'd spent almost seventeen years leading a perfectly normal and intrigue-free life—then *wham*. In a matter of days, everything had turned crazy.

I folded my legs underneath me and clutched my trusty spatula, the only thing there to protect me.

Well, I thought, *I only have myself to blame.*

Earlier I had insisted to Charlie, Daisy, Helena, and Susan that I had to complete this mission solo.

"It won't work unless I'm by myself," I had told them.

Typical. Typical! Now I was clinging to a spatula like it was my last friend on earth. I nearly laughed. All this for a purse. A purse that, I might add, I had strapped tightly over my shoulder. After all of this, I would probably never take it off again.

With jangling nerves, I glanced up at the clock. Where was Hattie? She was supposed to be back by now.

As the minutes ticked by, my anxiety started to increase. Then, out of the corner of my eye, I noticed a photograph on an end table in the corner. My curiosity got the better of me. What could a little snooping hurt? I stood up to investigate.

It was me, almost, framed three by five. I had an arm around Alfy Romero and my lips on his cheek. I gasped. I still hadn't gotten used to seeing Hattie like that—disguised as me. She had gotten it so right, down to the hot pink hoop earrings.

I studied her costume, trying to figure out what, exactly, made her look like me. She was wearing my glasses, had her hair long and wavy like mine, and was wearing my signature shade of lip gloss. But that wasn't entirely it. There was something else. I just couldn't put a finger on it.

And then someone put a finger on me. On my shoulder, to be precise. I yelped, but before I could whirl, there was an arm against my chest and a hand over my mouth. A lock of chestnut hair brushed my cheek.

It was Hattie. It was me. It was both. She'd snuck up on me. How had I not heard the door?

No matter, I'd slap her into oblivion with my . . .

I blanched. My spatula was still on the couch, leaving me defenseless.

Well, I thought, *this is it. At least I'm going to die with my handbag.*

"You!" she spat. She sounded almost scared.

I stared at the figure before me.

There Hattie stood, but it was hard to think of her as Hattie. Even I was drawn in by her convincing imitation. She glowered, shoulders thrown back, tapping the toe of her pink cowboy boot—exactly the way I would have if I was in her position. Hattie had Lulu pumping in her veins, but there was one problem. Hattie was a certified lunatic.

Because the most deadly weapon that Lulu Dark would ever brandish is a spatula, and even that she probably wouldn't use. Hattie-slash-Lulu, on the other hand, had gone straight for the knife-sharp letter opener that was lying on the desk.

Crap! Why hadn't I thought to Hattie-proof the place before putting my plan into action?

She brandished the thing, keeping it well within my line of sight.

"Tell me who you are!" she demanded. "Who are you? And why are you doing this to me?"

Her voice was pure anguish. This wasn't an act, I realized. Hattie was confused and scared.

I was defenseless. Worse, I was tongue-tied. Hattie stepped forward, the letter opener gripped tightly in her fist. This was it!

And then I had a flash of brilliance. Sometimes I surprise myself that way.

"Wait!" I yelled. As quickly as I could, I reached into my purse and pulled out my brand-spanking new driver's license.

"I'm Lulu Dark," I told her. "And you're out of your freaking mind."

Hattie recoiled like she'd been burned. She stared at the driver's license. There was my name and my picture.

You can't argue with paperwork. There was no mistaking it. I was the real Lulu Dark.

A panicked look crossed Hattie's face. She dropped the letter opener, letting it clatter to the floor. I contemplated my next move, but Hattie was ahead of me. She had hoisted open the window and climbed out onto the fire escape. All I could do was follow.

I jumped out onto the rickety metal structure and started clambering up in the darkness. I could hear Hattie a few flights above, racing up, up, up.

My eyes hadn't adjusted and I could barely see. I was feeling my way, stumbling, hoping that I wouldn't be too late. But too late for what? What was Hattie planning? I didn't even want to think about it.

When I finally made it to the roof, I caught my breath. Ten stories up, I found myself nestled in a canyon of lights. Halo City was twinkling all around, above and below. It was beautiful.

There was a full moon. Hattie stood on the edge of the roof with a crazy look in her eyes.

"Hattie!" I screamed. She barely seemed to register my voice.

"My name is Lulu Dark," she said dreamily. She didn't make eye contact. She was swaying back and forth on her heels. Slowly I approached her. I had to get her down from that ledge.

I wouldn't even want my worst enemy to jump off a building. But the weird thing was, Hattie wasn't my worst enemy—not by a long shot.

For one thing, no matter how creepy her obsession with me was, it was also sort of flattering. Hattie thought that pretending to be *me,* of all people, was going to bring her fame and fortune. And the fact that she was·drawn to me, the fact that she was able to impersonate me so flawlessly, had to mean there was a strange connection between us somewhere. An inexplicable similarity. In a way, she was my responsibility.

"Hattie, please listen to me," I began to say. I didn't want to make any quick movements that would freak her out.

"Hattie? I don't know who that is," she snapped.

"Just come down," I told her. I took off my glasses and looked her in the eye.

I thought I saw a crack in her armor, but she didn't move. Her lip was quivering almost imperceptibly.

"I'm Lulu," I told her. "You're Hattie, remember? You came from Motoropolis in January. Then you were Berlin for a while, but that wasn't real either."

"Stop it," she said. "I have no idea what you're talking about." Her eyes were watering.

"Yes, you do," I contradicted her. "I know these things. I am Lulu Dark. I can see through walls. I can see through you. And you can see through me too, enough to know that I'm not screwing with you."

Then she was crying silently, tears streaming down her cheeks. She turned her face away from me.

"Hattie," I said. "Look at me."

Crushed, she stepped down from the ledge and slumped on the pebbly surface of the roof.

She glared up at me. I could tell she was trying to be defiant, even through her tears. I reached into my purse and pulled out a Wet Nap. I used it to dab at my face—eyes first—taking off my makeup.

"I'm Lulu," I repeated. "This is Lulu. The makeup and stuff, it's nothing. It's meaningless. You can see through it just like I can, can't you?"

I felt a little dishonest there. I realized that I owed it to Hattie to tell her so. "The truth is, sometimes even I have a hard time remembering that the makeup, the cowboy boots, and the fringe don't matter," I said gently.

Hattie stared into my eyes. For a moment I was uncomfortable having her look at me like that—without my eyeliner and everything.

I bet I look like a little piglet, I thought, and instantly chided myself for being so shallow at the very moment that I was trying to discourage that kind of thinking.

I may have had my own misgivings, but Hattie was now transfixed, almost hypnotized. Knowing that it was time to strike while the iron was hot, I tossed her my whole packet of Wet Naps and then dug into my purse. I found the nameplate necklace and looked down at it. It glittered in my hand: *HATTIE.*

For some reason, I was almost sad to part with it. I'd been carrying it around everywhere, and it had become kind of a talisman. Even though I knew it was stupid, I couldn't help thinking that it had protected me.

I walked over to her, there in a heap on the ground. She was dabbing her face, wiping her makeup off just like I had. "Here you go," I said. I bent down and fastened the charm around her neck.

Then she was wailing in my arms. I'd never known myself to be such a caring person before, but I was rocking her, rubbing her on the back. Everyone deserves to have someone rub her back while she cries, even if it is her mortal enemy. Marisol and her mother had taught me that.

"Shhh," I comforted her. "It will be okay."

"No, it won't," she sobbed. "It won't be okay."

"Of course it will," I said. "I don't get what's so wrong with being Hattie anyway. For one thing, you're gorgeous. For another thing, you're smart, not to mention wily as a freaking alley cat. You have a sister who loves you, and, um, like the sexiest boyfriend in the entire universe. Who is head over heels."

"He doesn't love me," she cried. "He loves Lulu Dark."

"We'll see about that," I said. "Let's go back downstairs."

Hattie nodded dejectedly, and shuffled toward the fire escape.

Remembering something, I quickly whipped out my cell phone and sent Daisy a text message. Then I scampered down the metal stairs after Hattie.

When we climbed back through the window, everyone was there in Alfy's living room. Although I'd insisted on confronting Hattie on my own, they'd been just as adamant about waiting in the empty apartment next door—just in case. The message I'd sent Daisy was the signal for them to come out of the woodwork.

Hattie was still sobbing, and Alfy scooped her up into his arms. "I love you," he whispered.

"No!" She sniffed, pushing him away. "You want her instead." She pointed at me accusingly.

"That's where you're wrong," Alfy said. He took his girlfriend by the shoulders and gave her the sweetest kiss on the cheek before guiding her over to the couch. "You know the note that Lulu had? With my phone number?"

Hattie nodded.

"It wasn't ever for her. In the dark, on the stage, I tapped the wrong person. The message was for you. My roadie gave it to Lulu by mistake."

She looked up at him, still tearful but no longer crying. "Really?"

"Really."

I furrowed my brow. For real? I hadn't heard that part of the story. Now, *that* was kind of annoying.

"Ahem." Helena cleared her throat.

Hattie looked up suddenly, like she hadn't even known anyone else was in the room. As she glanced around—from Helena, to her sister, Susan, to Daisy and Charlie—it seemed to dawn on her that she was still in trouble. She was frightened again.

"I—I'm sorry," she stuttered. "I didn't mean to hurt any of you."

Helena and Susan wrapped Hattie in a group hug.

"It's going to be okay, sweet pea," Helena soothed. "I'll be friends with you until my dying day, no matter what you happen to call yourself. I've had several names too, you know," she added with a wink.

"And we'll get this whole Berlin thing figured out," Susan interjected. "I don't know how I'll do it, but I'll get you the best lawyer money can buy. I'm not going to let them send you up the river."

Hattie froze. "Up the river? You mean jail? Just for stealing her driver's license? And taking her parents' money and stuff? They can send you to jail for that?"

Susan furrowed her brows. "Well," she said. "Berlin is dead, honey. And the police seem to think that . . . well, they just wonder how she got to be dead and how you got to have all her stuff."

Hattie looked flummoxed. "I think she had a heart attack or something. I don't know. I met her on the train. We got to be friends during the ride. And we went down to the pier to see if there was anything fun. When we were there, she just, you know, had a spaz! Maybe she choked on one of the pork rinds I gave her."

"Pork rinds!" I exclaimed, remembering what I'd learned from

Berlin's school file. "Those are always fried in peanut oil. Berlin was severely allergic to nuts!"

"At least we're not looking at murder," Helena said optimistically. "There's only the little issue of fraud. But I'm sure Charlie's dad, the famous attorney, can make *that* problem go away." She looked hopefully at Charlie.

"Oh, sure," he said, "that's my dad's specialty."

"I did push Berlin into the bay and take her stuff," Hattie admitted sheepishly, shrugging. "But she was already dead."

"Well, don't do it again," Alfy said. He wedged himself back onto the couch and wrapped his arms around Hattie.

Daisy gave me a bewildered look. "Isn't Berlin—I mean Hattie— supposed to be the *villain?* Why are we all comforting *her?*" she asked.

She was right. Hattie had been through a lot, but the pity party was getting out of control. She was still seriously disturbed.

"There's also the matter of Hattie trying to push people onto the subway tracks," I said. "And purse stealing. And identity theft. And letter opener brandishing."

Susan picked up on my train of thought.

"You're going to have to go away for a little while, Hattie," she said softly. "To a hospital, though, not jail. You just need to take some time to sort things out. Get better. I don't want anything like this ever happening again."

Hattie buried her face in her sister's shoulder. "I know," she snuffled. "Me neither."

Charlie looked up, disappointed. "Does this mean we're not going to get to beat anyone up?" he asked.

"I guess not," I said.

"Rats. I've been practicing my karate all day," Daisy grumbled.

"I was looking forward to rescuing you," Charlie teased me. "My damsel in distress."

"I'm no one's damsel," I said. "Do you see me wearing one of those pointy hats?" Hopefully I wasn't blushing too hard.

"So, what now?" Charlie asked.

"Let's go roller skating," Daisy suggested. "The all-night rink is still open."

So we did.

THE END

IT WAS MY SEVENTEENTH birthday, and I was having the party to end all parties. I had invited everyone—I mean *everyone*—and to my surprise, they'd all shown up. Even Rachel and Marisol.

My dad and Theo were there, of course, and Helena, and Alfy Romero, and Jordan Fitzbaum, whose relationship with Rachel had blossomed in the few weeks since the Hattie incident.

Genevieve was there too, standoffish in a corner with her latest boyfriend, Vince, who, to my delight, seemed to be just as annoyed with Viking's yapping shenanigans as I had always been.

But everyone besides the dog seemed to be having a great time, and that included Rachel Buttersworth-Taylor. Marisol confided to me that Jordan had given her an ultimatum: be nicer or else. I had to say I was a little surprised at her for agreeing to such a thing. Yes, being nicer is good, as I'd learned for myself, but still. To change your whole personality just because a boy tells you he'll dump you otherwise? Someone get Gloria Steinem on the phone, please.

At least Rachel was following her orders starting with me. I didn't ever expect to be great friends with her, but at least we could coexist peacefully. Maybe even be friend*ly*. And I'd always be grateful to Marisol and her mom.

As for Hattie, she had left for the rehab center a week ago. And by "rehab," of course, I mean "the loony bin." The psychiatrists had prescribed a six-month stay, after which they promised that she'd be able to integrate herself into normal society. Alfy couldn't wait. He told her he'd visit her every week and send her a letter every day, and he meant it. Sally Hansen, I mean Lisa Whatever Her Name Was, had been wrong about him being a lying, cheating dirtbag. When he fell for a girl, he fell hard.

The other big news was that I'd gotten a job. No, it wasn't as an apprentice to Detective Knight. My days as a girl detective were done for. Instead, Helena Handcart was opening her own cosmetics shop, and she'd hired me as a part-time consultant. I couldn't wait to start.

The detective thing was still a sore subject because there had been a hugely embarrassing article on the front page of the *Halo City Times* just that Sunday. The headline had read: REAL-LIFE NANCY DREW SOLVES SHARK GIRL MYSTERY. I was utterly humiliated except for the part of me—the minuscule part, I might add—that was sort of proud. Inside, the *Times* ran a picture of me, Charlie, and Daisy sitting on a couch at Little Edie's, smiling.

No one would leave me alone about it.

Everywhere I went it was Nancy this, Sherlock that, and Angela Lansbury the other.

Dad and Theo were the worst culprits, of course, followed by

Charlie and then Daisy and Genevieve. Everyone seemed to want to get in on the act—mainly because they could see how crazy it made me.

Even my mom, who normally would never have noticed such details from my life, called from LA the day the article came out, just to torment me.

"Honey," she said in the low, sultry voice that was her trademark. "I have a mystery for you. I can't figure out what happened to my career. I was hoping that you and your chums could investigate for me. There must be a criminal behind it somewhere, and I suspect it's my agent. I need you to do me a favor and get him thrown in jail."

With my birthday party in full swing and with that conversation in mind, I approached Rachel, who had taken a moment away from Jordan and Marisol to get a piece of cake.

"Hey," I said, tapping her on the shoulder.

"Hey," she responded.

"Thanks for coming to my party."

"I love parties," she said. "It's nothing personal." She was joking, for once.

"I—I just wanted to say sorry," I began haltingly. "For the stuff I said about your mom, I mean. To tell you the truth, my mom's just as crazy. If not more."

"You don't have to tell me that," Rachel said, giving me a jocular punch on the shoulder. "I've seen that painting your dad did of her peeing in the sink. At least my mom knows what toilets are for."

I laughed. Rachel was somewhat hilarious—as long as you took it the right way.

"Anyway," she told me, "I'm sorry too. If I hadn't spilled that stuff on your skirt, your purse never would have been stolen. And the whole fiasco with Hattie would never have happened."

"Yes, it would have," I said. "Hattie-slash-Berlin had been following me for weeks, waiting to make her move. She was starting to run out of cash, plus she had to do something before her not-mom came to visit. So it was just a matter of time." I thought about it for a second, then decided to make a confession. Just to cement things.

"Plus," I said. "You can never, ever tell anyone this, but being a detective was kind of fun. I wouldn't want to make, you know, an *identity* out of it. But just for two weeks, I enjoyed it."

Rachel smirked. "I bet that's what they all say—right after they solve the Mystery in the Old Clock."

"Okay," I told her. "That's enough. And if you ever tell anyone I just admitted that, I'll track you down and kill you. Either that or put a dead fish in your backpack."

"Touché," Rachel said. Then Jordan snuck up behind her and grabbed her in a bear hug. Rachel squealed and Jordan planted a big smooch on her cheek.

Gag me.

I looked around the room. Jordan and Rachel weren't the only ones having a good time. Everyone was talking to each other and laughing and flirting. Perversely, it made me feel lonely at my own party. I wished I had someone to flirt with.

My eyes landed on Charlie and my loneliness evaporated. Charlie and I were still somewhere in limbo land after our night in the Dumpster. I'd been dying to ask him about it, but once again words failed me. We'd been hopelessly skirting the issue ever since. He was standing by the sliding door that led to the balcony, hair mingling with his long, perfect eyelashes. When he saw me watching him, he beckoned, and I followed him outside.

The late May air was perfect. There's nothing like a warm night with a blue sky. Full moon. Bright stars. Et cetera.

We stood there, surveying the busy street below us. Charlie pulled out a cigarette and moved to light it. Before he could, I knocked it out of his hand. He watched it fall to the sidewalk in dismay.

"What did you do that for?"

"Come on, Charles. It's so not suave. Didn't anyone ever tell you that you look like Bea Arthur when you smoke?"

"I don't even know who Bea Arthur is," he grumbled. He turned up his nose, but he didn't light another one.

I pressed my palms against the wrought iron railing, pushing myself up onto tiptoe, and leaned out as far as I could over the edge.

"School's over in a week," I said. "Summer is almost here. The possibilities are, like, so endless."

"Maybe another mystery?" he suggested.

"Yeah, right. I'm still getting over this one."

"You seem pretty recovered to me," he said.

I considered it.

"I guess the part that still freaks me out is the fact that Hattie was able to fool all those people. It was one thing for her to impersonate Berlin because Berlin wasn't even from around here. But she had everyone in Halo City thinking that she was me. It's kind of hard to stomach."

"Oh, you're exaggerating," Charlie chided me. "The people she actually tricked were people who didn't even know you. Like the Stratfords and Alfy Romero. But I would have known without a second thought. Daisy would have known too."

"I hope so." I sighed. "But I'm not so sure. Looking at her, dressed like me—in my exact same cowboy boots, the same glasses, and eyeliner, and lip gloss and everything—even I got confused for a second."

Charlie waved his hand dismissively and gazed out over the Halo City skyline. "That's just because you, and everyone else for that matter, are way too wrapped up in clothes and appearances and shallow stuff like that. It's so *silly*." At that, his voice cracked, and he gave an embarrassed laugh. He plucked a few petals from a potted geranium before speaking again.

"Let's face it. You're beautiful," he finally mumbled. "With or without your cowboy boots and makeup. But that's practically the least important thing about you."

"I'm beautiful?" I asked. I found myself grinning from ear to ear.

"Yes, you're beautiful," Charlie said softly. "Now get over it." He grabbed my hand and leaned in toward me. This time, nothing interrupted us.

ACKNOWLEDGMENTS I AM NOT TRYING
to be Elizabeth Wurtzel with the acknowledgments, but some people really deserve thanking.

Thank you to my editors, Margaret Wright and Kristen Pettit, for being reasonably patient and infinitely helpful, and for making *Lulu* a better book than I ever thought it could be. Thank you to my agent, Rebecca Sherman, for being my Jewish fairy godmother and for bearing with me through sweeps week. Thank you to Eloise Flood and everyone else at Razorbill for letting me write a book. Thank you to my friend and erstwhile psychic advisor, Jordan Schuster, for helping me with the Tarot card stuff—and for everything else, too. Thank you to my mom or else she will kill me. Thank you to Laird for being wonderful and steadfast. Finally, and most Wurtzel-y, thank you to Stevie Nicks—for the glitter.